TO LIVE

Chris
r
Steve

C. G. COOPER

"TO LIVE"

GET A FREE COPY OF THE CORPS JUSTICE PREQUEL SHORT STORY, *GOD-SPEED*, JUST FOR SUBSCRIBING AT CG-COOPER.COM

A HUGE thanks to my beta readers: *Mary, Kathryn, Michael S., Sue, Colin, Susan, Maggie, Michael F., Connie, Nancy, Sandy, Kim, Paul, Andrea, Melissa, Don, Gail, Richard, Len, Julie, Bob, Anne, Alex and Donald*. Thanks for watching my six...

And to my literary guardian angels, Paul and Glenda, thanks for everything :)

FROM THE AUTHOR

"TO LIVE" is a novel that came about after a handful of emotional conversations with my readers on Christmas Day 2017. What started as an outreach program to make sure no one spent Christmas alone, turned into a story in my head, and then a journey of soul searching that I hadn't intended to take. This novel is a work of fiction, but I hope it encapsulates the fear so many of us face in living up to our potential, and more importantly, I hope it highlights the brave life so many choose to live after the loss of a loved one. Because it is a choice; a hard choice with so many possible endings.

This novel is for the readers who have shared their stories, and for those who have yet to tell. Thank you for your honesty, your bravery and your incredible will to live. I've learned so much from you all. God bless.

- C. G. Cooper

PROLOGUE

Cancer.
Cancer
Cancer?

"Sorry, Ted, it sounded like you said cancer."

"I did."

"Oh."

Too many thoughts, most of all, relief. Strange.

"No time to waste. There are preparations to be made, things to talk about..."

The rest of the doctor's words faded into the background.

Just like that, it'd happened. A farewell physical on his last day of work, and here it was.

Elmore Thaddeus Nix rose from his chair. The doctor, his old friend, Ted Baker, handed him a pile of pamphlets. More platitudes.

"Sure, sure," Elmore said absentmindedly.

He passed by the nurse practitioner, the receptionist — even the other patients looked like they pitied him.

The pamphlets went into the waste bin next to the elevator doors.

It's better this way, he thought, pressing the button to go to the ground floor. Yes, it was better this way.

CHAPTER ONE

The house was stone quiet when he creaked in from the garage. That single step hurt. It was the knees. Who knew a step could send such pain streaking up a leg? There was a time when... well, that was another time.

Elmore Nix slipped off his shoes and set them next to the neat pile by the door. It's how Eve liked them, like soldiers on parade. Neat and tidy. Always tidy. Four pairs of his and only one of hers. The pair he'd bought at the discount place, the outlet mall she liked to go to on the way to Asheville. He couldn't remember the name.

"Mr. Nix, is that you?" came the voice from the kitchen.

"It's me, Martha." He followed the smell of chili. Martha was part caregiver, part cook. Good thing because the best Elmore could do was peanut butter sandwiches on white. Or burgers, if it was a Sunday and he was feeling gastronomically adventurous.

He padded into the kitchen, thinking that he should've slipped into his slippers, the ones he'd gotten two Christmases back. But there'd been that fall. (When had falls on hardwood started to hurt so much?) He huffed it away like so many things.

"How was your appointment?" Martha asked, stirring the pot on the gas stove.

"You know, another year, another physical." He glanced at the newspaper on the table. No interest there. "How is she?"

Martha let out one of those exhales. Elmore Nix had come to find that there were all manner of exhales. There was the exhale that marked exhaustion. There was the exhale that told you a person had had enough of a conversation. And then there was the current variety, somewhere between pity and hope.

"She's been tossing around a bit." Martha's southern accent rang clear when she spoke of her patient. "She's comfortable. Been askin' for you."

Elmore nodded. "Should probably get something to eat before I see her."

"I'll have it ready when you come back." Sweet Martha. Always knew what was best.

"Okay. I'll be back."

Elmore stepped lightly as he made his way to the other end of the house. The master bedroom had originally been a tiny thing, more of an afterthought than a real room. But, they'd knocked down a wall and combined it with the bedroom next door. She liked the view of the backyard. No less than four bird feeders and a birdbath out there.

The door was open, and he tried to ignore the harsh sounds of man-made machines used to keep his loved one alive.

He peeked inside, feeling like a teenager again, nervous and far from his sixty-seven years of age. She did that to him.

And there she was, sleeping peacefully. She'd lost weight,

but she was still beautiful to him. Always beautiful. His gorgeous Eve.

He stepped to the bedside, throwing a cursory glance toward the monitors. Interlopers. How many of these would *he* have? Maybe he could pull another bed into the master bedroom and they could lay their days away.

"Elmore?" Her eyes were fluttering open. She had that uncanny ability to always know when he was near. Even in a dead sleep, she'd wake and give him that little smile, like she did now.

God, she's beautiful, he thought.

"Hey Honey," he said, stroking her forehead, careful to avoid the oxygen tube.

"How was your last day, Elmore? I wanted to be there but Martha said I should get some rest."

She hadn't left the house in weeks. Still, she talked like she left every day. Not a shred of self-pity.

"It was good," he said. "They had cake."

"What kind?" she asked, the familiar sparkle coming to her eyes.

"Caramel."

She picked her head up. "From Benecke's?"

He nodded.

"Your favorite."

"Yep."

"Someone fudge the numbers in accounting to procure that?"

"Either that or there was a bank heist in town. Check the papers."

"Seriously though," she said hoarsely, "since when did those 'cheapos' ever shell out for a bakery cake for someone's last day?"

He wanted to tell her the good news. For some reason he didn't.

"I brought you home a piece."

She nodded, pretending along with her high school sweetheart. She hadn't had a bite of real food in five days – or was it seven?

I need to remember these things, he thought. *She would.*

"Did you put it in the microwave? Ten seconds?"

How did she do that? Remember every last detail of his life, right down to his peculiar affinity for slightly gooey caramel cake? She remembered things like that and he'd struggled to remember her shoe size. Now, he thought, he'd cling to these minutiae like the last piece of driftwood in a swirling sea.

"And was it perfect?"

"Hmm?"

"The cake. Was it perfect?"

"I should've had a second piece. Would have if you'd been there."

She nodded, knowing him better than he knew himself.

"Tell me everything," she said, placing her hand on his.

"Well, if you can believe it, I actually put all my stuff into a box."

A slight smile on her drawn face. "You didn't."

"Scout's honor. It was just like in the movies. They actually gave me a box. And so, I put in all my stuff – pictures, Post-its, my Elvis Pez dispenser, all of it. Plus a box of paper-clips – I had to take something, after all. And I walked out of that place with fifteen years of toil and tears crammed into a cardboard box. All I needed was a big ol' spider plant sticking out the top and I would've been the undisputed king of cliché."

He realized as he spoke that he would like to have stayed

for a full day of work. He hadn't missed a day in his life, not even when Eve got sick (she wouldn't let him). They went to the doctor on his lunch breaks or on the weekend. They were lucky enough to have a nearby seven-days-a-week place.

And as he spoke, he filled his soul with the sight of her. His wife. His beautiful Evelyn. The light of his life. His everything.

CHAPTER TWO

Eve died two days later, but not without imparting her final morsel of wisdom.

How had she found the strength, the will, to get the words out?

There he'd sit, trying to find the words. What could he say? How could he distill a lifetime of love into insignificant words?

Eve knew how. She'd done it.

But she'd messed up his plans in the process. She really had. But wasn't that how she'd lived? There were the dance lessons they'd paid for with the money he had put aside to restore his dad's old Pontiac. There was the trip to Paris with the money from the house extension.

Eve was always doing that – living in the moment. He was the planner. She was the free spirit, the light to his... well, to his life.

Those last moments he would never forget. Lucidity had been a fleeting thing for that last day. The meds kicked and swirled through her body. He could almost see it, smell it.

In those last moments, Eve just stared at him, with all the

love and warmth of their forty years together. Then came the moment of burning intensity, the glee for life she'd always shown. Those eyes burned right through him, filled him with hope that she was coming out of it. Maybe it had all been a mistake. There she was. There was his Eve.

Her hand tightened on his, lips moving, warming up for something.

"Live," she said, still locked onto his gaze.

"Okay," he said.

How could he break his promise? He had never lied to her. Never. He had never broken a single promise to her. Never.

Her eyes fluttered closed. Off she drifted. To sleep at first.

Devoted husband. Entranced partner. He sat, watching her chest rise and fall, until it fell for the last time.

Live.

CHAPTER THREE

He only left his house one time over the next week. The visitation was a small thing. Elmore didn't remember much, just faces he couldn't place, well wishes from strangers who had once been friends.

Then he retreated home. Her room was empty, but he could still smell her. He spent one day cleaning and purging. And then another, just sitting, staring at the bed.

And the rest of the time he slept.

And she came to him.

"Live," she said, and her voice was a whisper on his heart. "*Live*."

CHAPTER FOUR

A week after his wife's funeral, Elmore Nix finally emerged from his home. He was sick of refrigerated food. At least that's what he told himself. But deep down, it was Eve's words that haunted him. As the prisoner days passed, he felt that single word gain strength.

Live.

What had she meant?

Elmore tried to write it off as the last words of a dying woman, his dying woman, his love, his life. She'd gone and taken his life along with her. Their days together, their walks through the neighborhood. Not only had Eve been the center of every action he'd taken for the past forty years, she'd been the impetus behind meeting new friends, contacting old friends, and traveling near and far.

The sun spiked down, highlighting his exit as he pulled the car out of the garage. He'd forgotten his sunglasses. Too late now. Better get going.

He needed food. The stuff he'd received from well-wishers was almost gone.

Not that it mattered. Hunger was merely a biological

communication from his body to his brain. From his mind came a different message altogether: just wither away.

But there were two factions within Elmore Nix. While one faction would have him drown, the other would have him extract every last bit of oxygen he could from the water. And that was that. Giving up wasn't in the cards. Especially after the promise he'd made to Eve.

Live.

He ignored the turn for the grocery store. Too many memories. Shopping for summer vegetables for Eve's famous stew. Making a pharmacy pit stop for her weekly pile of meds. No. Too many memories.

He drove across town to a store he'd never been in to shop. It was a relatively new place, all clean aisles and fresh scents. Carts that went straight and not like Ouija board planchettes. A manager greeted him at the entrance.

"Good morning, sir," she said cheerily, stacking plastic baskets.

"Morning," he said.

They were the first words he'd uttered in days. His voice was coated in fuzz.

"Can I help you find anything?"

"No. Thank you."

She gave him a nod and went back to her task of running the store.

It took Elmore a few moments to orient himself. The place was huge, a sprawling center of American capitalism. Stacks of soda pop announced a merry weekend of revelry. A cooler of steaks and potatoes proclaimed the perfect meal for a God-fearing American family.

Eve would've liked the place. Fresh bread. Much more than their usual grocer. He almost asked for a pair of glazed donuts, something he'd done every Sunday. One for him...

Live.

He passed the bakery and kept moving. Still the memories. How was that possible? Every single thing brought images of her smiling face, her constant adventurous flirt. Eyes only for him. The images came like nuclear blasts blotting out the landscape.

He rolled past produce, wine, snacks.

Maybe a magazine, he thought. He liked the history ones, the ones packed with nuggets that he liked to chew on for days.

Yes, there it was. Aisle 12.

He scooted past a young family with a swaddled baby. The butcher gave the young child a tiny wave with a meaty hand.

The array of choices was staggering. There were magazines for everyone, with paperbacks on the far side. Not as many of those. Eve would've liked the selection. Pictures of far off places full of adventure and slim drinks garnished with wedges of fruit.

Move on, said the better half of his mind, as the other half let out its air and sunk a little deeper.

He found the history mags in a slot next to the gun periodicals. There was a special on Teddy Roosevelt. Teddy was one of his favorites. He grabbed a copy and started flipping.

One page, then another, and then another. It didn't stick, like he'd forgotten how to read. With a silent huff he replaced the magazine, searching for another. Nothing of interest.

In the midst of his search his eyes glanced left to make sure he wasn't blocking the aisle. No one there except a girl, maybe in her early teens - grabbing one card, then another from the greeting card section. He saw her giggle, replace the card, select a new one, and then giggle again.

Thank you cards, he thought. Eve would've done that. She sent thank you cards for the smallest things. He'd never understood it. Wasn't a verbal thanks enough? No, she would say. Sending a formal thank you was a solid contract of understanding between two parties. It was elevated. It was the way you behaved.

It was silly really, at least in Elmore's mind.

But now, there were the cards before him.

Something simple, he thought, for the friends who'd dropped off food. For the reverend of their church who presided over her service. Elmore didn't remember the words, but he was sure they'd been beautiful. The young man who'd become their preacher the year before had been Eve's favorite. Of course he had. He was young and full of energy. Sometimes too much energy for Elmore. Elmore was used to the endless drone from the pulpit. Now it was all hands in the air and smiles to the congregation.

Back to task.

He selected a plain stack of thank you cards. Good for everyone. No way did he want to stick around and pick a different one out for each recipient. A pack was efficient. A pack was cost-effective. Utilitarian. Here was the melding of his ways with her ways.

Satisfied, he placed the stack of cards in the empty cart. One thing done, he thought.

He pushed his cart around the girl who seemed to have found a card she liked. They didn't make eye contact. Such a thing wasn't done now. Now the name of the game was to stay in your own lane and stay glued to your smartphone. And that was fine with Elmore. This wasn't a social call.

But he couldn't help notice her furtive look, from the card to the rack. Then her hand reached inside a pocket of her jeans. Out of the corner his eye he saw the girl pull out a wad of bills. He guessed two, maybe three.

She was counting, and then looking up at the rack again.

He saw her shake her hanging head, place the card back in the rack, and then move past him.

Elmore watched the girl go. Why the pull? Who was she? No one he knew. But his gaze drifted from where the girl had disappeared to the card rack. The card she'd replaced sat askew. The label above the slot read: Get Well – Mother.

Live.

Elmore made his move.

CHAPTER FIVE

He rushed from the store, plastic bag in hand, thank you cards stuffed in his coat pocket. He scanned the parking lot. His body didn't feel like his own. He felt a tingling thrill. He'd never done anything like this. This was something Eve would do; not him.

Elmore found the girl sitting on the bench at the new bus stop, feet tapping on the pavement. He approached cautiously, clutching the grocery bag in his sweaty hand.

"Excuse me," he said.

She didn't look up, still tapping her feet.

"Excuse me," he repeated, moving closer.

Now she looked up and he saw the white cables running from her ears, the tail tucked into the folds of her clothes along with her hands.

She removed the bud from her right ear. "Yeah?" Wariness there.

Elmore held out the bag.

"That's not mine."

"Here," he said, reaching out further. Why couldn't he find the words? His mouth felt sandpaper dry.

"I said that's not mine."

Elmore took in the rest of the details now. Brown hair, slightly unkempt. Was that the style now? Blue jeans – were they even called that now? Torn bottoms. An oversized sweatshirt. He couldn't tell if she weighed under or over a hundred pounds. Thirteen or eighteen? No clue.

"I... I thought you might like it." The words sounded wooden and awkward to his own ears.

"What are you, some kind of perv?" The phone came out now like a blazing sword ready to save the day.

Elmore placed the bag on the ground and raised his hands to shoulder level. It hurt to go much higher.

"I saw you looking at the card. And I thought you might be thirsty."

She cocked her head, halfway to calling the police for sure. Then she looked down at the bag, nudged it with her foot.

When it didn't jump up at her, she reached down and pulled the card out.

She stared at it. Was it disbelief? Or more wariness?

She looked up at him, her eyes narrowed to slits. "What do you want?"

"Nothing. I promise. I just..." He closed his eyes and exhaled. "My name is Elmore Nix. I'm not a... a perv. I'm just... well, there it is. I thought you might be thirsty."

She reached down and pulled the Gatorade bottle from the bag now. He'd almost turned but found himself lingering. He wanted to see her reaction, good or bad. How could things get much worse?

But her face didn't harden; it crept toward the other end of the spectrum. Not a smile, but at least she'd loosened the death grip on the phone, had actually set it in her lap.

"I am thirsty," she said. "What's the catch?"

"No catch," he said, smiling. "Pay it forward."

He turned and started off. He'd done his duty for Eve. She would've liked the girl, he thought. Eve would've asked her about the music she was listening to, talked to her about riding the bus, which would've brought out the stories of how she'd taken a bus tour through Europe in college. That was Eve, not him.

"And thanks for the card," the girl called out when he was ten steps away.

He looked back. "You're welcome."

"It's for my mom," she said.

He chuckled. "Yeah, I kind of figured."

"You shouldn't go buying cards for people though. I'm just sayin'. Some people might find it a little creepy."

There was no wariness in that. And there was almost a smile.

And as he walked off, he recognized something. He analyzed it in the wake of echoes. Something in her voice.

A sadness that only the lost can feel.

CHAPTER SIX

Two more days at home. He didn't need much to eat. He'd found he wasn't as hungry as he usually was. He ate just enough to sustain him. Martha was gone, so it was all on him.

There were calls, luckily all by phone. No well-wishers at the front door. Another thing that wasn't done these days. Back when his mother had died, half the neighborhood came by every day for a month. He remembered his father had tried in vain to chase them off each time. His father – another long-lost memory that had stamped its presence on the soul of Elmore Nix.

"Time to clean this place up," he said to himself. He liked things tidy. Not in a compulsive way. It was just that tidiness simplified life. Elmore liked simple. It was easier that way.

And yet, as he picked up the broom, he thought of her, of Eve, his beloved. She liked to sweep. Imagine that. A person who enjoyed sweeping the bits of dropped life from the floor. He'd hold the dust pan for her after chuckling at the way she literally danced with the broom across the floor. He laughed because he knew she'd do it whether he was there or not. But when he watched her, her hips swaying to some tune that she hummed, barely audible, his heart danced with her.

What he wouldn't give for one more dance with her, one more body to body squeeze. The way his fingers sank slightly into the flesh below her ribs. And that awful ginger smell of that all-natural shampoo on her hair. How he hated it then. How he longed for its sharp sweetness now.

He'd made it all the way to the living room before he realized where he was. And it took him a few more beats to hear the knocking at the front door.

He set the broom against the wall. The knocking came again.

No reason to call out. The person on the other side probably wouldn't hear him anyway. He looked through the spyhole. It took a second to focus. The back of someone's head.

Go get the gun, he thought. *No, it's the middle of the day*.

Then the figure turned. He stepped back in shock. It was the girl from the grocery store.

He almost didn't open the door. Why should he? His part in her drama was over. He'd had no intention of cultivating the relationship any further than a random good deed.

But he opened the door anyway, slowly, cautiously, as if he half-expected the girl to leap nails-first through the screen door.

"Hello, Mr. Nix," the girl said, chomping on a piece of pink bubble gum that formed fractals of pink latticework between her teeth.

"Good morning," he said tentatively.

"Yeah, it's actually afternoon." The girl pointed up at the sun. "And a beautiful one. You really should be outside."

Elmore nodded. "How did you... is there something you need?"

"The Internet. You said your name. I just looked you up." She blew a bubble and sucked it back into her gaping maw just as it popped. "You should look into wiping your info from the search engines, you know. Some creep could steal your identity, and then it's years in legal costs. Happened to an uncle of mine. Nice house." She inspected the door frame.

"Thanks."

They stood in silence for a moment. The girl snapped another bubble.

"So," he said, "is there something—"

"I wanted to say thanks, you know, for the card and for the drink. You didn't have to do that."

The flutter in his chest made him steady his breath.

"You're welcome." Pause. What were the words? Then they came. "You know you could've called. If you found my address, then you found my number. Both are online."

She smiled. "You're right." Then she looked down at her phone. "But I..." She seemed to be gathering her thoughts, thinking of the right teen response. Something snarky maybe. Something meme-worthy. Wasn't that what the kids called it? But no "snark" came forth. "I needed to get out of the house, you know. Thought it might be a nice day for a walk."

She spoke the way kids her age speak – ending everything in a question mark. *Thought it might be a nice day for a walk?*

"Sure," he said. "A nice day for a walk."

She was avoiding eye contact now.

"Well, um, like I said, thanks for the stuff?"

A short wave and she was turning, already a step away.

"Did your mom like the card?" Elmore blurted.

She froze mid stride, her foot settling down in a careful maneuver of control. He thought he detected a slump of her shoulders and drop of her head. His father had called it the "I'm feeling sorry for myself" look.

"Yeah, she liked it."

"It was funny."

She nodded, saying nothing. He just stood there. Was the interaction over? What was the next move? Social interaction wasn't his forte, especially with teens. They were closer to alien beings than members of his own race. Elmore didn't understand their mannerisms, lingo, or choice in music. He didn't judge. Never that. He'd been judged, and he hated it. It was more like a person from the depths of Africa gazing on a person from the West for the first time. Totally foreign, a novelty, and an impossible bridge to cross.

The girl fully pivoted toward him, eyes still glued to the path, or maybe it was her feet. More fidgety hands.

"I lied."

Tingles ran the length of Elmore's arms. "Excuse me?"

"I said I lied. About my mom."

Elmore saw where this was going. He'd been scammed.

"You don't have a mom."

Her eyes shot up, angry at first, then understanding.

"No, I have a mom. It's just... well, she didn't understand the card, or at least, she didn't care."

He'd missed the mark. It wasn't the first time and definitely wouldn't be the last. But Elmore Nix was not one of those people who hammered themselves into pâté for getting something wrong. He simply recognized the mistake, learned the lesson, and moved on. Efficient.

"I don't understand," he said.

"My mom, well..."

Her eyes searched his. He wanted to look away. He was in uncharted territory. Eve would know what to do. He almost reached for the door jamb and called his wife's name. The awareness of her absence gouged him deeper than he would've thought possible.

The girl didn't finish her thought. Her mood had suddenly lightened. Elmore thought it was contrived; the teen putting on a brave face. But for what? "I've gotta go. Thanks again, Mr. Nix."

Again his mouth ran away like it had established a mind of its own.

"It's Elmore. I mean, call me Elmore."

She grinned. "I hope you don't mind me saying this, but that's a funny name."

"Which one?"

"Both."

"Elmore's an old name."

"Yeah, I got that."

"It's a family name."

"Yeah, well, you're like the first Elmore I've ever met."

Elmore Nix opened the screen door, took a step outside and stuck out his hand.

"Elmore Thaddeus Nix at your service."

She actually giggled, but she shook his hand. It wasn't the shake of a nervous teen, all tentative and loose as a wriggling fish. It was firm, dry, and fixed.

"It's a pleasure to meet you, Elmore Thaddeus Nix. Good Lord, that's awesome. It's even better to say it than to hear it. I'm Samantha. My friends call me Sam." She put one hand in her pocket and lifted the other to chin height. "Well, catch you on the flip-flop, Elmore Thaddeus Nix."

CHAPTER SEVEN

E ve would've liked Sam. Elmore found himself imagining the conversation they'd have about the girl. In his mind, he pretended that Eve had been gone when Sam came by, that it was his duty to fill her in on every detail. That was the way Eve lived. She poked and prodded, scraped away layers until she'd uncovered the beauty deep down. That's what she called it, *the beauty deep down*. His wife believed that fact with every ounce of her beautiful soul. She saw the good, through and through.

And now, as he had the silent conversation with his wife, Elmore picked the brief visit apart. The details of Sam's clothing, the way she spoke of her mother.

Elmore and Eve couldn't have kids. Eve said it didn't matter. He'd always been convinced that it was him. Maybe a by-product of his late teens or his time overseas.

Elmore had even secretly thought about getting checked out. His wife could be an amazing mother, a perfect mother. She had a seamless blend of outward love and the nurturing patience of a grade school teacher. She should've been blessed with a child in her womb.

"I miss you so much, honey," Elmore whispered to the empty house. He put his head against the cool wall, closed his eyes, and said it again. His grief formed a squeezing fist around his soul until it choked him.

He slogged away the rest of the day in silence, flicking on the television after dinner, then turning it off after ten minutes of running through the shows - their shows.

He went to sleep dreaming of Eve, of lost moments, of life alone. His last thought before fading to fitful sleep was falling down a deep well, far from civilization, far from help. Completely alone. The fading form of her on the opposite side of the bed faded a little more.

CHAPTER EIGHT

It was Sunday. The newspaper said so.

The newspaper had been a staple in their home. He always read it cover to cover while Eve did the crossword puzzle.

He couldn't make himself read it now. It dripped with so much memory that just the sight of it made him want to fall to his knees. Maybe he would call the newspaper and cancel his subscription. Maybe. Tomorrow he'd divest himself of all previous routines. Always tomorrow.

Freshly showered, Elmore stared at himself in the mirror. He was sixty-seven but still had the physique of a much younger man. Call it genetics. Call it the love of a great woman. Call it luck.

But beneath that exterior was the creeping disease. Cancer. He didn't want to think about it. How something so small could be eating away at his insides. He'd faced the fire before, but at least that had been something else he could see, confront head-on. But this, this was something different, something he didn't want to deal with.

He'd just bitten into his pitiful piece of toast, overdone,

not the same as Eve's perfect golden brown, when the phone on the wall rang.

He let it ring on and on before the digital voicemail picked up. He missed the machines, the kind you could listen to as a caller left a message. No listening in now. He'd been plagued by telemarketers as of late. The ringing stopped, then started again. He let it continue. It went through the requisite five chimes and then faded back to silence.

And then, it started again a moment later.

Elmore rose from the kitchen table and answered the phone.

"Hello?"

"Took you long enough, Elmore Thaddeus Nix. Good morning."

His face scrunched, then the strings on the corners of his mouth loosened into a tiny smile.

"Sam?"

"Bingo."

"I thought you were a telemarketer."

He heard the snort of a laugh, something both all-teen and all-Sam.

"I have a friend who stays on the phone with them and tries to get them to do all kinds of random things like bark like a dog and stuff."

"They're just doing their job," Elmore said. It felt good to talk out loud.

"Whatevs. It's still annoying."

"I thought you couldn't make calls from your phone." He didn't know why he said it. It was as close to a barb as he'd thrown in ages.

"Oh, I'm calling from a pay phone."

"They still have those?"

"Of course they do. We don't have flying cars yet."

That made him laugh.

"I sure would like to see that."

"Yeah, like in *Back to the Future*."

"That's a little old for you, isn't it?"

Her voice came over with a hint of haughty condescension.

"Are you kidding? Marty McFly and Doc Brown are my jam."

"Your jam? Is that a good thing?"

"Oy," she said.

Silence seeped into the gap. He wondered if they'd been disconnected.

"So, what are you doing today?" she asked.

"Just *putzing* around the house."

There he was again, using Eve's words. *Putzing*. He couldn't remember using *putz* in a sentence since calling someone a *putz* in grade school. He didn't know whether to smile or feel uncomfortable at the long-forgotten word.

"Yeah, me too."

"I thought you said you were on a pay phone."

"Oh, right." He could almost see her chewing the inside of her cheek. "I just went out for a walk."

Where was this conversation going? If he was a cynic, Elmore might've thought Sam was trying to get something out of him. But he couldn't afford to be a cynic, not with so much grief.

"A walk sounds nice," he said, again with the blurted words.

"Yeah, it's a beautiful day." Pregnant pause, then, "Wanna come with me?"

The question stunned Elmore to silence.

"You still there, Elmore Thaddeus Nix?"

The recitation of his full name snapped him from his

shock. It was what his mother had called him, both when she was proud of him and when he was in trouble. It was a good way to give a kid a complex. But coming from Sam's lips, the incantation sounded like some sort of ironic joke.

"I'm here," Elmore said, scratching his stubbly cheek. How many days had it been since he'd shaved? He'd never missed a day to shave. Not since his high school days when there wasn't even anything to shave.

"Well, what do you say?" Sam asked.

"What do I say to what?"

"To a walk, jerk face."

"Oh, well..."

"I'm not asking you to take a mortgage out on your home, Elmore Thaddeus Nix. I just thought..."

"Okay. Where should I meet you?"

"I'll come to your place. That okay?"

"Sure."

And then she was gone. No goodbye or anything.

Elmore didn't know how long he'd been standing with the phone to his ear, until the dial tone shook him from his meanderings. The receiver went back in its cradle and he just stared at it, scratching his scruffy cheek.

CHAPTER NINE

I t usually took five seconds for Elmore to choose his clothes for the day. Not that there was much of a selection. Eve had tried to add variety to his wardrobe, but it was one of the few things he'd resisted. He preferred practicality. Function over fashion. Plus, when you limited your selection, say from one to three options, there was no hemming or hawing about what to wear.

But this morning, after a good shave, Elmore stood over his pulled-out drawers and stared. He couldn't compose himself enough to pick a T-shirt or button down, shorts or light pants?

With a huff, he closed his eyes and let blind hands do the choosing.

He was dressed, hair combed, and waiting on the front porch when she arrived.

"Elmore Thaddeus Nix!" she said with a wave, like they were college buddies.

"Morning, Sam."

"Which way should we go?" she asked.

Elmore had thought this through. Walking his neighborhood wasn't the answer. While he didn't socialize with most of his neighbors, they knew him by sight. They might wonder what an old man was doing going for a walk with a teenage girl. He imagined explaining that she was his granddaughter, or that she was a niece thrice removed, but he couldn't lie. If it came down to it, Elmore would tell the truth: she was his friend. Zero in common and no physical attraction.

If that was weird, then fine, he was weird.

"The park?" Elmore offered. There were plenty of people at the park, but most people kept to themselves and their families.

"Sure."

So they left the well-trodden streets of Elmore's neighborhood and headed west. The park was a ten-minute stroll along a smooth, white sidewalk.

Along the way, Sam jabbered on about who knew what. Elmore found himself just enjoying her bubbliness, her utter lack of fear regarding their limited relationship.

"Do you think we can keep walking?" Sam said when they reached the park entrance.

"You don't want to go in?"

"Yeah, I mean, well, I like the sidewalk, and there aren't all those kids learning how to ride bikes."

Elmore scanned the park path and didn't see a single tot learning to ride on wobbly wheels. But he didn't argue. Elmore Thaddeus Nix didn't argue.

"Of course."

So they kept walking.

Every once in a while, he chimed in with an "Oh," or "That's nice," and even an, "Interesting," but for the majority of the near-hour-long walk, it was Sam who filled the silence.

She was an alien speaking an alien tongue, and he was learning by phonetics.

She talked about school and how she hated it. But she got good grades. Her favorite subject was history. He said he liked history, and for a time she went on about the Constitution.

"Ever wonder how bad it must have smelled during the summer at the Constitutional Convention in Philadelphia? I mean, they didn't have deodorant back then. They had powder. And they wore those damned wigs because they didn't wash their hair. And their breath stunk. Probably not Franklin. He spent a lot of time in Paris, you know, and, like, probably learned a lot from the French?"

"I always wonder," he said, his weary old voice falling like a feather in the air, "about the precarious position all those men were in back then. Each of them wore a potential noose around their neck."

She turned, her eyes wide. "Right? Could you imagine wondering if you were going to be murdered just walking back to your hotel? Oh, and did you know Thomas Jefferson invented mac 'n' cheese?"

"He didn't exactly invent it. He brought it back from Italy."

"Still," she said, holding out her arms like a balance scale, "Mac 'n' cheese, the Declaration of Independence... I don't know..."

The memory came in a cold splash. Something he hadn't thought about in ages. He'd been as nervous as he could remember. It was all he could do to keep his entire body from vibrating like a tuning fork.

He, in his pressed uniform and she, in her pink summer dress. She smelled like flowers picked from the freshest meadow in the universe. His palms were sweaty and his brow flushed, but Eve hadn't seemed to care. She'd been the one to grab his hand first. It sent a bolt of electricity up his arm that he still remembered, like sticking his hand into a toaster.

It happened like this. A crack in the sidewalk or a waft of something in the air sent him down a tube back in time, immersed him into a pool of recollection. One insignificant detail leading to another, more significant one. Until he was there, feeling everything there was to feel back then, heightened now by the prickling sensitivity of hindsight.

His mind was cast back thirty, forty years. Eve. So beautiful. So full of life.

Life.

Live.

"Elmore?"

"Eve?"

That was when the real world came back with a snap. He was walking on a sidewalk. And it wasn't Eve walking next to him.

"It's Sam," the girl said.

"Right, sorry."

He thought she was going to let it go. Everyone lets slips pass by like a fart on the wind. But she didn't. She waited a few paces and then asked, "Who's Eve?"

His body winced, though he was proud that his face didn't. He hitched a breath and answered.

"Eve is my wife."

"Oh," she said after a moment.

They walked on - an old man fading into the sunset and a teenage girl rising with the moon. He envied her until he didn't. He'd lived a full life, a good one.

"Is it okay if we find somewhere to sit?" Elmore asked.

"There's a bench over there by the pond."

They strolled to the pond, Elmore's legs doing their best not to wobble. Had it gotten warmer? Suddenly he felt like it was stifling.

They took a seat. A cardinal flitted away at their approach.

Sam was saying something, maybe commenting on the lack of ducks or the general disarray of the pond, but Elmore didn't hear it. It was like she was speaking at the bottom of a well whose entrance was covered in insulation. She was all warbles.

Something flew across his field of vision and he flinched. What was that?

More muffled sounds. He looked all around. Clarity shifted to blurs. Back and forth.

He didn't see but felt his hand grip the park bench. He didn't feel but saw the world falling away but he wasn't afraid. This was it. This was his time. He was going to see Eve and he wasn't afraid.

CHAPTER TEN

B*eep.* He was having such a wonderful dream. Eve was running along the beach chasing their first dog, Eddie, a border collie. She dodged the waves and sloshed through foam as they touched shore.

She kept waving to him, her smile lighting the world.

He reached for her on more than one occasion, but found that she was just out of arm's length.

Beep.

The dog plunged into the surf and Eve jumped up and down, hands clapping. He stepped closer, reached out again. Still no contact.

Beep.

She turned, flashed him a grin – her grin, the mischievous one, the one that had hooked him and pulled him along for countless adventures.

"Come on," she said, motioning to the waves. She waded in up to her knees. The dog was well out, past the breakers now.

Beep.

He spoke, but the waves broke around the sound. He was trying to tell her that the water was too rough, that it looked like a strong undertow. He saw the subtle signs, the shift of water toward the west end of the beach. He had summers on the Keys to thank for that insight.

Beep.

Eve turned and plunged into the first waves, water cascading over her body. Fully clothed, she plowed ahead.

Then the edges of the world collapsed and he felt himself falling. He looked down at his feet and found that his legs were buried, the sand sucking him up to the hips now.

He tried to call out, tried to scream for his wife. But she kept plunging, long sure strokes after the dog. And then she went under like a diver.

Beep.

CHAPTER ELEVEN

He moved his lips, careful at first. They felt like a ruined landscape.

"Elmore?"

That voice. Why was it so familiar?

"Elmore?" it said again.

He tried to blink. Why couldn't he blink? Had he lost his vision? Why would God take his vision just as he'd entered Heaven? And why did he feel so thirsty? Shouldn't he feel sated, feel a perfect sense of appreciation for the life he'd just left?

"Elmore."

His eyes worked this time, batting to life. The light stabbed. It hurt. Slowly opening his eyes, Elmore took in the sterile whiteness of a hospital, and these flashes of white painfully seared his vision.

"Elmore Thaddeus Nix."

Then he remembered. The girl. Sam.

"Sam?" he said, his voice no better than the croak of a baby frog.

He felt someone grip his hand.

"It's me," she said.

His vision was clearing blink by blink. All he wanted was to go back to his dream, back to Eve. But he'd been raised better. His grandmother always told him that you never ignored anyone, especially a friend, no matter the circumstance. She'd had all sorts of rules. Yes, sir. Yes, Ma'am. Tuck your napkin just so at dinner. Never have more than one dollop of jam on your biscuits.

"What happened?"

"You fainted."

He saw her now, her face painted in fatigue and worry.

"I did?"

She nodded. "How are you feeling?"

"Alright," he lied.

Her face was about to break. "Why didn't you tell me?"

"Tell you what?" he managed.

She looked around, as if about to utter a secret password. "The big C?"

"Cancer?" he asked.

It was the first time he'd said the word to anyone but himself. He hadn't been back to the doctor since the day of his diagnosis. His grief had superseded any other self-awareness.

"They said you were dehydrated, by the way," she said. "That's why you blacked out."

That made him laugh. He'd been dehydrated before, but not in the normal world. He'd learned his lesson then and almost made it a point to drink a glass of water every hour. He was as regular as the day was long.

"Now we know cancer can't trump thirst."

Sam didn't approve of his dark humor. He wanted to explain it away as the babbling of an old man who'd seen better years and now just wanted to be left alone.

But that would've been a cruel spear thrust into their budding friendship. But did he really have time for a friendship? He had dying to do.

"When was the last time you had something to drink?" she asked. She sounded as sure as any nurse he'd met.

"Well, I... You know what? I can't remember."

He expected a jab like "You really should take better care of yourself," but no lecture came. Sam just sat next to him, her hand on his. He keenly felt its warmth.

"How long was I out?"

"Not long, an hour maybe. You kept going in and out."

"Like a broken television," he said, grinning, trying to insert some levity, trying to make her smile.

"It's not funny," she said.

He nodded; his manner returned to grave and serious. "Of course it's not. I'm sorry if I scared you."

That's when Sam came back. She shook off a portion of the worry and did her best to smile. However, like a healthy mother touching a leper, he could still sense her trepidation.

"I had to borrow your phone," she said, pointing to his cell phone that lay on the bedside table.

"That's fine."

"You don't have many numbers in there."

"I don't?"

"Most people have fifty, maybe a hundred."

"Really?"

"I know a girl at school that has the phone number of every kid in our class.'"

"Impressive."

She was stalling, filling time and empty air with words. Elmore let her do it. The fact that he felt lousy didn't equate to trying much harder.

Sam nodded absently.

A nurse and doctor duo passed by not giving the room a glance. Elmore wanted to ask when he'd be released, but something held his tongue. He felt it coming like the thunder of a herd of buffalo over that far hill.

"How bad is it?" Sam asked. He knew what she meant. Why was everyone afraid of the word?

Elmore shrugged, tugging the IV in his arm. "I'm okay."

"You're not okay. She leaned in, voice lowered. "*You have cancer*."

He stared at her and those inquisitive eyes. Why did she really care? That's what he wanted to ask, but didn't.

He tried to explain it in calm and soothing terms, but the words felt like they came out like a jumbled bag of jellybeans.

"It's... well, it's hard to explain, is all."

"Are you having chemo or radiation?"

"You have an opinion on which is better?"

"Don't be a jerk. I'm just asking."

"I'm weighing my options."

Sam's eyes went cold. "I don't believe this."

"Sam, I..."

Before he could get another word out, she was up and walking briskly to the door.

Can't I just die in peace? he thought.

CHAPTER TWELVE

The emergency room doctor sent Elmore home with clear instructions. Drink water.

Thanks kids, Elmore had wanted to say. He empathized more with the middle-aged nurse standing next to the pubescent doctor. Her look said, "You better take care of yourself, old man, because you're not crowding my ER with your negligence." He respected that. Gruff determination and control.

He took the bus home. He would've walked, but his head still ached and the nausea came and went. Best not to push it.

A DAY WENT BY, then another. No call from Sam. No impromptu visit. He didn't know her number or where she lived. Not that he would be that brazen. Elmore Nix believed people come around in their own time. At least the best did.

On the third day of being cooped up, he folded the newspaper and shoved it in the recycling bag in the garage. He was bored. Plain and simple. Bored to tears, to death – to everything.

He chuckled. *Bored to death*. Now that was a thought.

Eve could sit and stare at a shoreline for days and still not get bored. She soaked in every detail while he sat by, the dutiful husband, trying to match her enthusiasm.

He *putzed* around the house for an hour, rearranging the coffee mugs, sweeping the kitchen floor, then moving to the storage space over the garage. Too hot in there.

The sun outside twinkled through the curtain. He pulled the drapes aside. No one walking by. No mailman with a bundle of junk mail to add to the Nix mailbox.

Outside. That's what he needed. When he'd gone to fetch the newspaper, he'd noticed the flower beds needed tending. That was Eve's job, or at least it had been. He'd done the heavy lifting, hauling bags of mulch, peat moss, or whatever Eve had ordered from the store.

Yes. Tending the flowers would get him some much-needed fresh air, clear his thoughts, and maybe get a sweat going.

He changed into his yard work clothes, the same pair of jeans he'd mowed the lawn in for twenty years. The things still fit his trim frame after all this time.

After gulping down a glass of water, and filling a bottle for later, he grabbed a pair of gloves and Eve's tools from the garage and set to work.

He made short work of the weeds, which thankfully weren't plentiful. Just enough to make the place look shabby. Then came a quick job of pruning with his skilled hands. He found he lacked his wife's artistic ability. It made sense. Elmore Nix was the utilitarian of the two. Sometimes Eve would shape their boxwoods into interesting shapes or maybe even an animal that would last the season. The best he could do was a round of tidying.

He was just moving on to the side yard, where the shadow

of the house shielded sunlight from a row of anemic plants, when he noticed a figure.

She lifted a hand chin high. The other was jammed into her pocket.

"Good morning," he said.

She just stood there.

"Sam?"

Still no words. He fidgeted with the trowel in his hand. What do you say to a teenage girl who's staring at you?

"I'm sorry for leaving you at the hospital," she said.

"That's okay. I'm not your responsibility."

"No, but there's a way to be, like a person, you know?"

"It's okay, Sam."

She shook her head like she wanted to explain. "Hey, do you need any help?" she asked instead.

Elmore looked at the pitiful plants on the dour side yard. He was almost finished. "You sure you want to get your hands dirty?"

"Dirt is my middle name."

"Your parents were creative with that one."

Her face brightened. "Hey, look at you making a funny!"

There she was again, the Sam he'd come to enjoy as a sparring companion.

"Grab a pair of gloves from the garage, you nitwit. I've got plenty of tools here."

She nodded and headed towards the garage, something of a skip in her step. Her eagerness was back, her enthusiasm for spending time with him, Elmore Thaddeus Nix.

But instead of being happy that she was back, instead of enjoying the moment, all he could think about was why a young girl would choose to spend her days with a withering old man.

CHAPTER THIRTEEN

He got up and stretched his legs one calf at a time. He'd had runner's legs once, but time had put an end to that. Now he was left with limbs that cramped in payment for half a day of tending the yard.

"You should get some new tools," Sam said. She was holding the hose out as far as her thin arm could manage and was washing her hands with it. "Seriously. Go to Home Depot or something. The ones you have are ancient."

"I like them. Besides, they work just fine."

Sam bent down to douse her face with cool water.

She blew a spray of water. "Yeah, but the new stuff makes it so much easier."

He found that she knew something about gardening. She was gentle with the plants and ruthless with the weedy inter-lopers. She handled a spade like she'd been born with one and arranged mulch with all the deftness of a card shark. He hadn't asked where she got her talent. Maybe a class at school. Maybe her mother or an aunt liked to garden.

"Why are you here, Sam?" he asked, watching her wipe her face with the bottom of her oversized shirt.

She looked at him. "Huh?"

"Sam."

"Yeah?"

"I said, why are you here?"

She looked around. "Um, I'm helping with the yard?"

"That's what you're doing. I want to know why you're doing it."

Her gaze shifted to her feet. "I like spending time with you."

"But why? I'm an old man."

Now her eyes met him, twinkling back. "Right, you're a crusty old fart."

"Cut the crap, Sam. I'm sixty-seven years old. Some people would say this is a little weird. I don't mind it, I'm saying. But, you know, people get ideas."

"It's not weird. You're not a creep and I'm not... well, I'm not into that stuff. Look..."

Her mouth froze mid-sentence. Then closed. And then she gave a shrug and smiled.

"I'm not asking because I don't want you here. Truly. But shouldn't you be with your friends? Family?"

It was the truth. What teenage girl in her right mind wanted to spend the day, or multiple days, with an old man with half a leg in a grave?

"I... I don't..."

"What is it, Sam?"

Tears filled her eyes.

She looked as though she wanted to run. And she did. She ran the five feet into his arms.

And she sobbed.

And for the first time since Eve's death, he felt something.

It was something she'd said once while they walked on the

beach with Eddie. The dog had plunged into the water and was knocked over by an unexpected breaker. She started to run toward the dog like a mother. Of course, the collie was fine. A little worse for wear as far as pride was concerned, but fine.

But he noticed the look on her face. And he asked her about it.

"I was afraid there for a second, that I'd have one less thing in this world to care for. I'm of no use when I can't do that."

He thought of this now, with the love he was feeling for this girl, Sam.

Finally, he was of use again.

CHAPTER FOURTEEN

"Sorry I got snot all over your shirt," Sam said, picking at the corner of her sandwich.

"It's okay. I was already a mess."

After the cry session, *sans* explanation, they'd gone inside for a late lunch. He made ham and cheese sandwiches warmed on the Williams Sonoma panini press he'd given Eve for Christmas five years before.

They went on with their meal, not speaking, digesting in more than one way.

When they finished, he wordlessly rose and collected the dishes. She followed. They coordinated washing and drying as if in a Zen-like trance.

"My mom," said Sam. "She's sick."

"I kind of got that idea from the get-well card."

"Not that kind of sick. She's, well, it's embarrassing."

Sometimes the best words are no words at all. Elmore focused on stacking dishes in the drying rack.

"She's an addict," Sam finally said, mopping a towel around a glass.

"I'm sorry."

Sam nodded, setting the glass on the counter and grabbing another. "It's not good, at home I mean."

Why the card? He wanted to ask. No prying.

"You're welcome here any time," he said.

"Really? I've only come here unsolicited like every single time."

They worked on. With the dishes done, Elmore fussed in the pantry while Sam stood at the kitchen window, just staring out.

"Sometimes I wish she would just die," she said suddenly. At first, he thought he'd misheard.

Elmore understood. He'd thought the same thing about his father.

He set the can of chicken noodle soup next to the tomato soup. "Sam?"

"Yeah," she said without turning.

"Look at me."

This time she turned to face him, a brave face. He saw right through it. She was on the lip of that dark precipice, the tears waiting in the wings.

"Tell me."

"I can't. She wouldn't want me to."

"Who am I going to tell?"

He motioned to the empty room, but really, he was motioning to his empty life. No job. No friends. No wife.

She looked around absently. Then walked over to the kitchen table and crumpled into a chair, face in hands.

"It's terrible," she said. "And it's embarrassing."

Elmore took a seat next to her.

CHAPTER FIFTEEN

"So, I guess it begins with Dad," she said. "He was a rep for Motorola and would leave every so often to negotiate contracts, right? Well, one time, he left and never came back. It's gonna sound weird, but like, I wasn't really hurt by it. Don't get me wrong, it was totally awkward, him not coming home and Mom getting all riled up and making calls and crying at night for a week. Anyway, after a while, she starts going out at night with her girlfriends. You know women, right? The minute something happens, they all flock to the rescue. I was, what, ten? I knew it then. I didn't question it. Mom would go out and tell me to keep the doors locked. I'd stay in, watch TV, and eat a tub of frosting. Pretty soon, she was staying out all night and coming home smelling like she'd fallen into a pickle barrel. And looking worse. She was, what do you call it? Classically beautiful? Is that what you old people call it?

"Anyway, on the nights she made it home, she'd always made it a point to tuck me in. She smelled like a cocktail. I actually like the smell of alcohol on the breath. It's sick-smelling and warm, but I like it. That's an alky in the making,

I guess, right? Whatevs. She'd tuck me in and kiss me and say something slurred. Then, she'd shuffle out of the room and I'd hear the sound of ice in a glass. All friggin' night. But here's the deal – there was something so sweet about it. So tender and loving. Someone sloshed like that and they're obviously hurting and fragile and all that love is like an exposed nerve. Anyway, we went out to eat a lot. And at home it was just the two of us. We were BFFs, you know? Rented movies. Her drinking actually slowed. I mean, it started at five sharp. But I guess she was like steady with it? It wasn't a problem. I guess that's the recipe for it getting worse. No one's paying attention.

"Then there were her boyfriends. Good Lord, some of them were toads. She first started introducing them as coworkers. First, they stayed in the car while she tucked me in. I would hear her leave and get this nauseous feeling in my stomach, like something awful was going to happen to her. Then they started coming into the house. I guess she wasn't trying to hide her shame anymore. You get to that point. There was an endless friggin' parade at one point. These gross guys who couldn't take their eyes off her ass even as they patronized her daughter. I liked it better when they just ignored me.

"Now, keep in mind, I'm just, like, eleven? And I'm starting to think about who the hell I am. And so when she leaves at night with one of these dirt bags, I get out of bed, hit the fridge, and start texting my friends. I'd hear the car pull in and jump into bed and all was well. Mom once told me she felt like she was in college again. I felt the same way. I mean, I hear that's what it's like in college. You're free. I loved it. And then Dad showed up, and everything changed.

"I was the one who answered the door. He stood there looking like a Jehovah's Witness. He cocked his head to the

side. 'Hey, pumpkin," he says. Like I'm five. Mom told me to
stay in my room. She was nice about it but I resented it. I got
real close to the door. I heard everything. The old man had
gotten remarried, had two kids, and settled down. He'd
gotten a desk job. No more traveling. There was a lot of
yelling after that, mostly from Mom.

"He said there was a third baby on the way. And he said
he was tapped out. He couldn't afford child support. Mom
went apeshit. The thing is, he was citing these loopholes, like
the fact that Mom was spending a lot more time with me
than she used to, and the fact that his new job was paying
him less. And so, he had these legal rights and stuff that
would allow him to pay a lot less. Mom accused him of not
reporting correct income. It got ugly. But part of her gave up.
I heard her tell a friend that she couldn't afford to fight him
with lawyers.

"That's when the party really came to our house. After
that visit. Friends, neighbors, random people off the street.
Mom started pawning stuff. If my father had paid for it, she
got rid of it. The bedroom set, the coffee table, even the
coffee maker. We were left with an empty house. At least she
let me keep my things, but I suspect a couple of things that
she said were broken were sitting on a shelf somewhere in a
thrift store. I knew we were in trouble when the stack of mail
got bigger. Angry letters. That's what I called them. Letters
from lawyers. Letters from real estate agents. The day I saw
the letter in my dad's handwriting was the same day I found
the pills in my mom's purse.

"I don't know what they were, but I know the bottle
didn't have her name on them. She was a nurse then. I knew
she'd stolen them from a patient. There's more. A lot more. I
just, well, I don't want to say them out loud. Do you ever get
the feeling that if you explain something out loud, like some-

thing that happened in the past, that that something will happen again?

"Yeah, so I won't bore you with the rest of the details. In summary, Mom and I live in whatever motel will take our credit card of the week. I think the cards are probably swiped. She hasn't had a steady job in close to a year, and I'm sure the next time I go 'home' we're going to be homeless. And that's that."

SOMETIMES, the only thing you can say is nothing at all.

So that's what they did. They sat at Elmore's kitchen table saying nothing for a very long time.

CHAPTER SIXTEEN

Sam was a daily visitor now. Now that Elmore knew the reason why, he was careful to be as welcoming as he could without making it seem like charity. He knew Sam wouldn't like that. She was the type that could sniff out pity like a hound dog catching the scent of steak a mile away.

He made the meals, and she washed the dishes. Sometimes they watched old movies, and other times they played Scrabble, which Elmore loved because it reminded him of Eve. She'd been the best, rarely picking up the Scrabble-approved dictionary for help.

Elmore never took it easy on Sam, and she seemed to appreciate that. He loved the way she'd stew over a particularly hard mix of letters. Sometimes she'd make him laugh with the choices. Words like "syzygy". He hadn't laughed this much since, well, a long time ago.

WHEN ELMORE LOOKED BACK, he wondered how he hadn't seen it. Life could be ruthless, and that was the only certainty about existence – that it always found a way to sneak around the corner and sucker punch you when you weren't paying attention.

And so it was with one beautiful Tuesday on the block. He'd just finished the day's crossword puzzle - save for three words that Eve would have polished off for him.

Here came Sam walking down the block, backpack swaying from side to side. She had her earphones in. He could always tell if it had been a good day by whether she had her earphones in. Good day meant white cord. Bad day meant cord in the pocket.

White cord.

He eased out of the rocking chair, thinking that a healthy snack might do Sam some good. He had no idea what she ate at school, or if she ate. Perhaps she was on assistance—he hadn't asked and she hadn't offered. What he did know was that Sam never left a crumb on her plate. Even when he made something that he was sure she hadn't liked, like the gumbo he'd spent an entire morning cobbling together, she still ate it all and most times asked for seconds.

The man at the grocery store had been helpful. When Elmore asked what he should get as snacks for his grandkids, the clerk had been more than happy to supply a bevy of options. Those options now lined the pantry.

He selected a bag of trail mix with M&Ms in it and poured half of it into a bowl. Even though he'd told Sam that she could have the run of the place, she never once went in the pantry unless he asked her to fetch something.

He set the bowl on the table and grabbed a Sprite from the fridge. He personally avoided the stuff. The sugar didn't settle well anymore. Another one of life's jabs. At least he wasn't wearing diapers yet. Maybe next week.

Sam came in the front door without a knock. At least she

was comfortable with that. He'd told her it was silly for him to greet her every time, like she was an infrequent visitor.

"Elmore Thaddeus Nix," she called from the front of the house.

The constant recitation of his full name made him smile every time. If anyone else had said it, even the woman behind the counter at the DMV, he'd cringe.

"I got your mail," she said, stepping into the kitchen, tossing a handful of envelopes onto the table. She already had taken off her backpack and left it inside the front door, along with her shoes. When he'd let slip that Eve mandated a shoe-less house, Sam had made it a point to remove them every time.

She peeked into the bowl. "This doesn't have raisins, does it?"

"It's trail mix," he said. "Of course it has raisins."

She snorted derisively, grabbed a handful of the stuff, and shoveled it in. The way her cheeks puffed like a squirrel getting ready for winter made him wonder if she'd eaten at all.

"You got more than usual today," she muffled around the mix.

The mail-getting was a recent development, one he was heartily grateful for. The weather was getting nicer, and there were more of his neighbors outside enjoying it. He'd found himself dreading the idea of their eyes pitifully filming his every move.

"What's that one," she said, reaching for another handful. "That thick one on top with a cool logo."

Sam was into her second handful of trail mix by then. He wandered over to the pile, a gun-shy recipient of well-wishing cards. He saw the symbol on the envelope. It was more like a crest.

"It's nothing. Junk mail."

"Doesn't look like junk mail."

"Probably one of those AARP knock offs. Just wait until you're old enough to have your own place."

"Huh. You know, I got one of those AARP letters when I was like seven. My mom thought it was hilarious."

The chuckle he forced out *sounded* forced, at least to his own ears. It was a verbal mask he could wear to hide the languid tones beneath it, one that fooled no one.

"I'll make sure I shred this along with the rest of them," he said, scooping it off the top of the pile. He couldn't get to it fast enough.

That's when she leveled him with the stare, the curious one, the one that told him she wasn't going to forget. "I caught you," the stare said. It was only there for a second, but he saw it.

"So, how'd the crossword puzzle go?"

He exhaled as quietly as he could, stuffing the envelope in his back pocket.

"Not bad. Maybe you can help me with a couple words."

CHAPTER SEVENTEEN

Lightness was returning slowly to his life, stamping out a piece of darkness with each passing day. For the most part, he still wallowed, and when he caught himself at it, he widened his eyes and breathed deeply – the very act of feigning wakefulness kept him awake. And he busied himself.

His internal alarm clock still woke him up at five on the nose every morning. Routine these days had transformed Elmore from a self-pitying clutch of the past, to a man making a concerted effort at restructuring his life. He'd rise, use the bathroom, brush his teeth, and drink a full glass of water. Then he'd lace up his shoes for a walk around the neighborhood.

The pre-dawn walks often brought back a flood of memories, most of them good ones. He loved the peaceful desolation of the early streets, the bruised tint to the sky, his footsteps light and dreamlike. Around six a.m. came the guy in the beat-up Chevy chucking papers onto driveways. Elmore regarded the Chevy's appearance as a harbinger of the normal person's daytime, and that's when he began his re-acclimation into the world of non-dreams.

This morning was like all the others, but he'd decided to walk a little farther, maybe leave the neighborhood altogether. He'd decided his watch held no meaning for him on this morning. If he was going to be arbitrary about space, then dammit, he'd be arbitrary about time as well.

He left the neighborhood far behind. A sheen of sweat glossed his brow by the time he made it to the park, the one he'd first walked to with Sam. Aside from this and a twinge of thirst, he was grateful for the fact that, for the most part, his old body complied. No creaks. No need to slow down.

Not the same for his mind, and so, he eased the able body onto a park bench and watched the sun come up. Tangerine first, then lemon.

As the sun crested the horizon and splashed the landscape, he felt the flood of emotion. The tears came and he didn't brush them away.

I let her finish your crossword... I didn't mean it...

He stared at the sun. He watched it cut away from the horizon, steady as the day.

"*Live*," said the sunrise. It whispered in her voice.

He nodded, pushed himself off the bench, and once again agreed to her request.

THE WALK back home had taken more out of him than he was used to.

He vowed right then and there to walk like that every morning. No morning funk. Just walk.

He made it home just before seven. He was just pulling the keys from his pocket when he saw her standing on his front stoop.

"Sam?"

She whipped around, hand still in the air mid knock.

A look like relief, like panic subsiding. "You scared me," she said, quick to retrieve her arm and her composure.

"I took a little detour."

"Yeah, well, I thought I'd stop by before school."

"I can whip up some breakfast if you want."

He didn't know when her school started. He'd never asked. Hadn't seemed important. Their friendship was an afternoon one, not a morning one.

"I already ate," she said. He could see it was a lie to avoid having a friend go through the trouble.

He unlocked the front door and led the way in, flicking on lights as he passed. What he really wanted to do was kick off his shoes and sit down, but he could sense the excitement – or was it urgency? – in the girl's demeanor.

"What brings you here this early?"

It was all the prompting she needed, a balloon ready to pop.

"The letter, the one with the crest, or I mean, the drawing of the medal on it."

The words hit him like a spear in the spine. On his way to the kitchen, his foot caught the edge of the carpet, right at the lip, the spot he'd promised Eve he'd have someone fix. He caught himself on the door frame.

"Whoa, you okay?"

"I'm fine," Elmore said, shaking off the unease.

"So that letter..."

She was chewing on the inside of her cheek, searching his face. He knew what was coming, braced for it as best he could.

"Elmore," she said, "why the hell didn't you tell me they gave you the Medal of Honor?"

CHAPTER EIGHTEEN

His mind traveled back for what felt like a thousand years, to another time, another life. He didn't like to go there, but Sam's question had dropped him down the silver tube of memory.

There was metal in his mouth. He tasted it like chewing gum.

"You need to leave," he said in a voice that wasn't entirely under his control.

Her mouth opened, attempted to form a word, and then closed.

He recovered himself just enough for politeness. "Please, Sam."

Her eyes stared, as if she hoped there'd be more for him to offer. When it became obvious that there wasn't, she said a plaintive, "I'm sorry," and walked away toward the door.

He knew she was sorry. He wanted to say he was too, but that wouldn't have been true.

The door closed with finality.

And Elmore Thaddeus Nix sat down in his well-worn

armchair - the one Eve had splurged for on his sixtieth birthday. He sat there and he watched the wall until he was aware that his body was shaking. Then he cried.

CHAPTER NINETEEN

Morning turned to night, turned to day.
The phone rang and was left unanswered. Three knocks on the front door, or was it five?

Food had no taste and his bed brought no solace. He slept on the couch, cranked neck and all. He would've slept on the floor if he'd thought he would've been able to get up afterward. The floor was solid, unmoving. He needed something like that in his life, something that didn't surprise him. He'd had too many surprises recently. All he wanted to do now was to be left alone.

And so he sat and waited.

For what? Death? Sam? A miracle?

A miracle came on the morning of day five with the sound of a battering ram smashing his front door to smithereens.

CHAPTER TWENTY

He'd been in the bathroom when the thought came to him. His trips to the bathroom had decreased as he missed mealtimes. Using the bathroom was a matter of propriety, a vestige of his civilized self. There was no sense in messing the furniture that someone else might get after he was long gone.

No, the bathroom was much cleaner.

He'd do it in the bathtub with a straight razor. The cleanup would be easy. Why hadn't he thought of that before? So simple. No muss, no fuss. Hell, they could just cart the whole bathtub out if they needed to.

Suddenly, his mind had eased, and a hole in his gut had healed in that moment. He almost smiled at the thought. Here was a plan. Here was purpose.

Staring at the bathtub, mind reeling in nourishment-deprived delirium, he heard the first crash and he thought it was thunder.

Thunder. That's strange. It was sunny when I came in here.

Another crash.

Then the thump of steps, though he tried to tell himself it

was more thunder, or maybe the pounding was from fist-sized hail.

"Elmore?!"

The call came from the front of the house.

It was her.

"Eve?" he called back weakly.

He stumbled back a step, his rear bumping into the sink. He steadied himself and blinked through the sudden blur in his vision.

"*He's back here,*" someone said.

The bathtub was rising now, along with everything within his vision. He steadied himself again when the world began to drip in reverse. He tried to stave it off, willed his legs to flex.

He was lying on his side when they came in, Sam first.

"What the hell happened?" she said, frantic.

"Where's... Eve?"

"Hang in there, Elmore Thaddeus," she said.

Then another face appeared, somehow familiar.

A man – a hard look. No, not hard, *determined*. A face as old as Elmore's, flinty and chipped.

"What have you gotten yourself into now, Nix," it said.

It was the voice of a dead man.

"Franks," Elmore said. His voice creaked. "Sergeant Franks?"

"That's right, you crazy devil. Come on now."

He smiled. *Death wasn't so bad after all. Sergeant Franks had come for him. Why not Eve?*

No time to ask, because Elmore Nix's world faded into shards of black, and then everything went quiet.

CHAPTER TWENTY-ONE

Whispers on the wind. That's what Eve called them. The soft titter of children on the playground wafting on the breeze; little laughs cute enough to bottle and take home for safekeeping.

He heard them now – the whispers on the wind – as he floated in a sea of bliss.

He became aware of other sensations. A prickling of the skin. So, this is what liberation of the soul felt like.

He also became aware that his eyes were closed. *Strange,* he thought, that he should be aware of his earthly body in this manner. *Should he open his eyes? Would there be light?*

There was light – hard, piercing. He forced his eyes open despite this.

"Well, look who's condescended to grace us with his presence again."

The voice again. The gravel of a lifelong smoker.

"Franks?"

"Right again. Give this man the lollipop prize."

Elmore's vision wavered for a moment, then cleared.

There was Franks, different somehow than when he'd appeared in the bathroom. What was it? Ah, the stethoscope.

"Hold still, Nix, I need to make sure you're not going to keel over again. Glad I still have some things from my EMT time."

The cool steel touched his chest. Franks removed the plugs from his ears and slipped them down to his neck.

Sam appeared. She was keeping her distance like he had something infectious.

"You had us worried, Nix."

"I... how did you..."

Franks threw his stone-cut chin behind him in a gesture toward Sam. "It was this little lady here. She called me, said she hadn't seen you in a few days. Thought you might need help."

He wondered only for a moment how it all fit together – how Sam knew Franks. *From that damn letter.*

Why wouldn't they leave him alone?

"I heard about Eve," Franks said. "I can't tell you how sorry I am. I lost Jenny a few years back."

"I'm sorry too," Elmore said. His voice was a rusty whisper.

Franks turned to Sam.

"I told you there was nothing to worry about, young lady. Nix might be as stubborn as a white-tailed pig on Sunday, but he's as healthy as a horse. Once we get some fluids in him."

One question stuck with him. Why hadn't Sam called an ambulance?

Franks threw his chin in the direction of the IV line. "You know, the last time I saw you hooked up to these many wires..."

"Leave it," Elmore said.

Franks paused. "Y'always were an ornery one."

It made Elmore remember, all the jibes, all the kidding. Sergeant Franks could be as mean as they came, but under that gruff exterior that trained countless young men, was a soul as kind and as pure as you could meet.

"How did Jenny die?" Elmore asked. He didn't know why. It wasn't really appropriate. He never would've asked someone on the street or even a co-worker at the job he'd just retired from.

But Franks was from another world, another time, when asking the hard questions was considered proper. Not just proper, your duty.

"Drunk driver." Franks shifted the sheets so they covered Elmore's upper chest. "Went cold turkey after that. Not a drop. Can't even stand the smell of the stuff."

"I'm sorry."

"You said that already, Nix. And besides, we don't say sorry, remember?"

Elmore did remember. Franks had said it long ago on a battlefield. "Never say you're sorry for what you're about to do. They won't understand, and you might not either, but you never say you're sorry."

It was those words that had gotten Elmore Thaddeus Nix through it all.

He caught sight of Sam in his peripheral vision. She stood staring, unmoving, arms folded.

"You wanna grab me a glass of water from the kitchen, young lady?" Franks asked.

"Sure," she said without affect.

Franks looked down at his old friend. "I didn't want to say this in front of her. You're looking pretty rough, Nix. What's going on? And while we're at it, why haven't you answered our letters?"

The letters. More in recent years.

"That part of me is gone," Elmore said, dreading the fact that his words would have no impact. He knew Franks. The man wouldn't let the episode go for a second.

"We're family, Nix. Maybe not by blood, but what the hell is blood anyway? We're family."

Shame shadowed Elmore's vision. His family. His first, really. He'd become a man with them, had nearly died for them – would have died for them.

"There aren't as many of us as there used to be. Oklahoma Joe and Tidewater Teddy died last year. Went out kicking though. Had a party for each of 'em, right there in their hospital rooms. Damnedest thing you ever saw."

Franks shuffled to the other side of the bed, checking the IV he'd placed. He was older, but still the same Franks. Those resolute eyes and that always-set jaw. It was a face of tested confidence.

"So, what about you, Nix? How's life?"

Elmore actually laughed, a full laugh that shook the bed. It went on for a good thirty seconds, maybe a minute. Sam rushed into the room and stared down, uncomprehending.

"Is he okay?" she asked.

"Oh, he's fine."

Elmore knew the word for what he was going through. It belonged to Franks. A joy burst. When you've had a crappy day, a crappy week, or a crappy life – and suddenly everything comes out. And it's not a scream or a tear, it's just a burst of craziness, like your body finally realizes the ludicrous way the world works. Joy burst.

Elmore got his laughing fit under control, though everything in the room made him laugh. The look on Sam's face. The tube stuck in his arm. The sight of his old friend, mentor and hero. Another bark of mirth escaped his lips.

The pained look on Sam's face told him that she was

trying in vain to share in the experience. She edged closer and closer, and eventually took a seat at the end of the bed.

"Whelp, now that we've got our good friend Nix here under control, why don't you enlighten me as to the nature of said friend's discombobulation, and the origins of your own budding friendship."

CHAPTER TWENTY-TWO

"What can I say?" said Sam. "It started with a card and a bottle of Gatorade. Who would stop and think that those two things – what do you call them? Innocuous? Like, how could those things form the basis of... anything? But he gave them to me and it... I don't know. It made me think there was some good in the world after all."

"Don't make me out to be some sort of savior," said Elmore, who wanted to add that the gesture was merely the pathetic attempt of an old man to conjure up the memory of his late wife.

"I thought he was batshit," she said, letting a shade of a smile creep onto her face.

"You wouldn't be the first one," said Franks.

"I had nothing better to do, so I stalked him and came to his house. He was nice to me. Now he's just Elmore Thaddeus. He's like a fa— whatever, he's just a good guy."

"So," said Franks, "you two seem to be doing just fine. How about we move on to business? My letters."

"It's about the Medal of Honor, right?" Sam said.

"It sure is," Franks said. "You know what they give those out for."

"Yeah, I did my homework. It's presented for acts of extreme heroism. It's the highest award bestowed by the president."

"Ding, ding, ding. Give that girl a golden ice cream cone. We just call it the Medal. That's all. The Medal."

"And he got it, right?"

Again, the cringing sensation took over Elmore's body. He wanted to disappear. They were talking about him like he was some museum exhibit on display.

"He sure did. And let me tell you, I was there when he earned it. Hell, I wrote him up for the damn thing."

"Really?"

"Really."

The memories, they flooded in now. Not the images of mangled bodies and ripping mortars, but strange things, things he'd never tell another human being. The silence, most of all. The thought of catching your breath before one last run for cover. The sight of the midnight moon minutes before a firefight. The soft chatter of men in the foxhole next to you, talking about their farm back home, their dog, their girl.

He loved the beauty of it. That's what he would never tell. He'd gone off to war a boy, fully expecting to die. He'd found himself, but he'd found beauty as well. The beauty of a man crying for his brother. The beauty of a man causing his brother to excel. The beauty of life and death. There was no finer struggle. And there was nothing else in life to find.

Elmore Thaddeus Nix came home to a conflicted nation. But rather than push his memories away, he embraced them. He had no choice but to do so. They made him whole.

Then came the medal. Lowercase m. The medal ruined everything.

"That's right, Sam," Franks was saying. "Our friend Nix saved my ass and the asses of one hundred and seventy some shit-stained Marines."

CHAPTER TWENTY-THREE

"So, what's the letter say?" Sam asked.

Elmore barely heard the question. They were coming faster now, the faces of his long-ago friends. Cincinnati Steve, Charleston Charlie, and his favorite, Jersey Joe.

He, along with Sergeant Franks, had been the only ones without a nickname. Nicknames made time pass. Nicknames simplified everything. When you told stories about Cincinnati Steve, it was about all the funny or stupid things he'd done. If you called him his real name, Steven Romaninski, it made it all too real. For boys in muddy trenches, plodding one weary foot in front of another, war was like playtime - scary, deadly and profound - playtime, but still detached from the real world. It was "the disconnect" from that world that sent so many of Elmore's comrades to their deaths afterwards.

"The letter's an invite, Sam." Franks was looking at Elmore now, that damn NCO stare, the one you couldn't look away from. It spoke to your foundation, struck you right in the soul's jugular. The stare played on Elmore's conscience now more than ever.

"I'm not going," Elmore said with a flat voice.

"Yep," said Franks. "We've sent Nix a letter ever year for the last twenty and the old soldier hasn't answered a single one." He turned to Sam now. "Can you believe that? Elmore Nix, nicest guy you've ever met, the glue that kept us together, silent as the grave."

A crow clacked outside and Franks turned to look out the window.

"What's the invite for, Mr. Franks?"

A slight smile appeared on the man's face. To Elmore, it was a look of contempt.

The eyes glared hotly at him, and the man said, "We want to say thank you."

CHAPTER TWENTY-FOUR

Nighttime.

Franks was gone, but Sam remained. She'd called her mother to say she'd be home late. No apparent dissent there. Elmore didn't ask. He never did. Sam's business was Sam's business.

"Eggs and toast good for dinner?" she asked. "It ain't a five-star meal, but I'm pretty good at it."

He was feeling better now, more like himself. The fluids had restored him. Like sloshing water that tasted like iodine from a dented canteen. Rain you couldn't drink. Streams swollen to fill rice paddies. Plodding along in waterlogged boots, praying to make it to the next checkpoint, then much closer to a beer with the boys.

"Yo, Thaddeus, you with me?"

"Eggs and toast is fine," Elmore said, walking away from the bed. "And yes, I'm with you, Sam." She was staring at him again. He didn't like it. They'd been equals and now he was the old man. How had the tables turned so quickly?

Right, the damned letter.

"Wanna give me a hand?" she asked, motioned to the kitchen.

"I think I'll sit and watch."

He'd just taken a seat at the kitchen table when he noticed that someone had cleaned the kitchen to a nearly acceptable standard.

"We need to make a grocery run," Sam said, head buried in the fridge.

"I'll go tomorrow," he said, though he didn't much feel like it.

Sam went about cracking eggs, stirring them until the stovetop was hot enough. Then she sliced in some butter and cooked away.

The eggs were a little overdone, the toast a little under, but it was food, and his body craved it. Before he knew it, he was asking for seconds. There was plenty. Sam had made enough for six people. He plowed through it, surprised by his ravenous hunger.

"So," said Sam, "are you going to go or what?" The girl knew how to lob a whopper across the table.

"I said I'll go tomorrow."

"I'm not talking about the grocery store, dopey."

He leveled her with a "let it go" stare. It didn't work. She was Sam and he was Elmore Thaddeus Nix.

"You know what I'm talking about. They just want to honor you. Forget honor. They just want to say thanks. Why don't you want to go?"

How could he explain it to her? It wasn't that she was decades younger. It wasn't that she was a girl. It wasn't even that she hadn't been to war. He would've told the truth to Franks if given the chance.

"I don't want to go. Can't we just leave it at that?"

"No." She sat back in her chair and folded her arms. She looked like a mother grounding a disobedient child.

"It's just a bunch of fuss, Sam."

"Yeah, but it's not about you, Elmore Thaddeus Nix. It's about giving them the opportunity to thank you. Are you just scared to be in the middle of it? Is that what it is?"

"Sure. I hate being up on stage. Stage fright."

She didn't catch his lie. "We can work on that. I can help." Her wheels were turning now. He could see it as plain as if her face were made of glass, revealing the cogs and whirls of her mind behind it.

"I don't want to go, Sam."

"We're going."

He shook his head. "Excuse me. *We?*"

She smiled, a look of triumph. "Ye-ah. I'm, like, going with you?"

"Who said?"

Her smile broadened. "Mr. Franks said I could."

CHAPTER TWENTY-FIVE

S am left at a quarter past seven. And Elmore sat in his living room wishing she was there. He wanted to tell her. He wanted to tell her everything.

But this was his age-old dilemma. He was the stoic. That's what Eve called him. He never complained or made a fuss. Eve would rib him for that, saying it wasn't natural to keep it all in.

Even Eve didn't fully understand.

ELMORE THADDEUS NIX enlisted in the United States Marine Corps at the age of seventeen, in 1968, just after the Tet Offensive. His peers were running for the border, entering Canada, asking for college deferments, basically doing anything they could to stay out of uniform. He knew one young man who stood in the middle of the high school gym class, hoisted a forty-five-pound weight over his head and slammed it on his foot. That had worked, but the guy had never walked the same again.

Elmore didn't remember much of the process. He did remember that there seemed to be a certain excitement amongst the Marine recruiters. "We've got a live one," he heard them say from a back hall where he waited to get checked out by the Navy doctor.

His mother had a fit. She railed and cried. He tried to hug her, tried to make her understand, but he didn't even understand himself. It was some kind of compulsion, a pull he couldn't fully explain.

So, he went to boot camp. Parris Island should've been one of the worst experiences of his life. The drill instructors were cruel, pushing their charges to extreme exhaustion and sanity.

But Elmore Thaddeus Nix, now Recruit Nix, sleeping in the cot closest to the squad bay door, finally felt like he belonged. Parris Island was his awakening. It happened all at once. He was home at last. There was the screaming spittle and thousands of push-ups, but he was home.

Here he was judged by his actions, by his successes and failures, not the failures of his father. No, these drill instructors, these sadistic bastards, were tearing him down and building something else in its place. Elmore might've been the first in his platoon to really understand it. And it probably wouldn't have played out that way if it weren't for his bladder.

In the middle of the night he rose to hit the head. Swift and stealthy he went. The Marines were America's ninjas, able to slip by a battalion just to take a squirt.

He'd been halfway through his relief when he heard the crying. At first, he thought it was one of his fellow recruits. He knew them all by their names, born given and DI given.

Recruit Nix strained to hear the location of the crying. It was coming from the squad bay. It was coming from the air vent. It wouldn't be the first time curiosity pulled him to a revelation.

He cut through the squad bay, nodding to the recruit standing watch. The kid was almost asleep on his feet. He made a show of caring, but it was obvious he didn't.

Recruit Nix charted the path as best he could. He didn't know why. The sobs could've been a recruit from another platoon or another company. A couple of turns and he heard it – the sobbing of someone who didn't want to cry but couldn't help it. The involuntary spasms of human grief.

And then he was there, staring around the corner at two drill instructors, one with a hand on the shoulder of a Marine whose body shook, his head buried in his hands. It was his drill instructor, Sergeant Stacks, who was doing the crying.

"He's gone, Gunny..."

The gunny was their company gunnery sergeant, a man named Stillwell who'd already done two tours overseas. Gunny Stillwell was a living legend standing among mere mortals. Even officers gave him space.

But at that moment, he wasn't the towering figure the recruits had come to know. He wasn't doing one-armed pull-ups or hauling an injured recruit out of a fighting pit with one chiseled arm.

"I'm sorry, son," he said.

"He was my brother, my best friend."

A nod of understanding from the demigod. More crying from Sergeant Stacks.

"This won't be the end of it. You know that. They'll bring his body home and you'll grieve. You'll hold your momma's hand and toss dirt into that hole. But you just remember this, that's not him. He's a Marine, goddammit. And just like the hymn, your brother is standing watch now, guarding heaven's gates."

Sergeant Stacks looked up, his face twisted in grief. "He don't belong in heaven, Gunny. He belongs here."

"I know, Marine. But God's got a plan for all o'us. And shit, it ain't for any o'us to decide what it is. C'mere, son."

Then the larger Marine did something that Elmore would never forget, something he saw time and time again when he did his own tour of duty. The war hero, the tough as nails Marine who probably called generals by their first names on the golf course, stepped closer and hugged that grieving drill instructor. Like a father. Like a brother.

The next day, everything was back to normal. Sergeant Stacks was the same mean old cuss he'd been before Recruit Nix witnessed his undoing, but now Recruit Nix, and more importantly, Elmore Thaddeus Nix, understood the yin and yang of the human psyche.

He graduated somewhere near the top of his class. Recruit Nix was motivated, but not too motivated. Any smart Marine recruit understood that lesson. Never highlight yourself. Never volunteer. The Marine Corps would highlight and volunteer you for plenty. No need to help the Green Machine.

Elmore arrived at Parris Island a mixed-up kid with a half-assed mission in life; he left a Marine – a changed man. With his eagle, globe, and anchor, he departed with the first real sense of who he was at his core.

HE SMILED AT THE MEMORY. Not one in a hundred Marines would admit to loving their time at boot camp, and he would never admit it out loud. And there were days when he was lost in some long-ago memory, that he envisioned going down to the recruiting station now. He could still do at least ten pull-ups, had decent mile run time, and knew his way around a pushup.

But such fantasies were merely the backwash of memories that could never be retrieved in the flesh.

Time to sleep, Recruit Nix, he thought to himself.

But he didn't go to bed.

As he floated off to unconsciousness, his memory of the Marine Corps melded with Eve's words.

Live, Recruit Nix. Live.

CHAPTER TWENTY-SIX

School precluded Sam from coming over the next morning. That didn't mean she couldn't call. And she did, precisely at seven a.m.

"Elmore Thaddeus Nix, did you make a decision?"

"You mean about breakfast?"

He could imagine her rolling her eyes.

"No, about the letter. You need to tell Mr. Franks whether you're going."

Oh that. But of course he knew what she meant.

"I haven't decided yet."

"Well you better hurry. I'm sure they're waiting to hear. And you don't want them to go to all the trouble if you're not coming."

Right. All the trouble.

"Don't you have homeroom to get to?"

"We don't have homeroom, Elmore Thaddeus Nix. Jeez, what are you, like, a hundred years old?"

It made him smile.

"Almost, Sam."

He heard her laugh, probably tried to muffle it with her hand.

"I've gotta go. Okay if I come by after school?"

"Sure."

———

HE BUSIED HIMSELF THAT DAY. Swept and mopped the kitchen floor. The fridge gleamed and the counter sparkled, he moved on to the next room.

Around the house he went, leaving a path of clean tidiness. He lingered on the guest bedroom. Memories there. Best not to think on those now. He passed it by, moved on to the master.

He'd made it to the living room when he saw the envelope with the invitation, sitting on the coffee table right where Sam had left it. It was overloaded, stuffed with who knew what. They seemed to get thicker with time. The same deal each year. The logo stamped on the outside. That blasted medal.

He figured the invitation just got thicker, fancier, like they sourced it from some faraway forest where only the rarest trees were good enough to give up their lives for a Medal of Honor recipient.

He passed the duster over the coffee table, avoiding the envelope like it might catch the feathers in a puff of fire. Around and around he went, thinking.

It was all in the past and Elmore wanted to leave it there. But if it was in the past, how could it hurt him now?

He made the final call on his fifth pass around the room. A neat, barely perceptible ring of dust still surrounded the bulging letter. He set the duster on the floor, no need to get the table dirty again. Then, ever so gingerly, he picked up the envelope and flipped it over. It was heavy, weighted with a pre-stamped envelope, no doubt. Leave it to a pseudo-government organization to pay too much for paper. What a waste.

Do it, something whispered. He looked all around as if he might be caught in an incriminating act. *Open it,* the whisper said.

Elmore shivered. He was going crazy. That had to be it. The cancer was eating him from the inside out. Well, if that was the case, maybe he wasn't even standing in the middle of the living room staring at a bloody envelope like a lunatic.

Before he knew what he was doing, the envelope tore open. No saving the packaging like he did, even with junk mail. No, sir. This one ripped in a diagonal corner to corner.

Like Charlie Bucket unwrapping his golden ticket, Elmore Thaddeus Nix stared down at his deeds. There was the thick casing of paper in his hands, but it was just another package. There was the embossed logo, the officious proclamation so familiar and yet so foreign.

But it wasn't this letter, the one from some brigadier general Elmore didn't know. It was what was inside the womb of the official letter that pulled him in. Note paper, yellow, white, crumpled in places and torn in edges, uneven and imperfect. A stack of them. It felt like dirty trash in Elmore's hands.

So, cast them away, he told himself. *Nothing to see here.*

He just stared.

And then he unwrapped them and laid them on the table, one by one. Familiar names and barely legible writing. He paused to steady the flow of adrenaline in his limbs that made him want to bolt from the house and never stop running.

Read.

So he did. He read them all, and his life cascaded back to a time when there was a distinct purpose to Elmore Thaddeus Nix's existence.

CHAPTER TWENTY-SEVEN

The day he arrived in Vietnam, three men in the very platoon Private Nix was reporting to, died.

They were having a memorial ceremony when he and five other freshly-shaved grunts and their gear arrived at the battalion headquarters. All six just stared and stood at an uneasy attention. Private Nix caught sight of one of his new companions, a pizza-faced kid who looked no more than fifteen. The boy was trembling. And so were a couple of the others.

Private Nix didn't shake. He didn't cry. No, he just stared, absorbing what he could. Weary troops with tear-stained faces lined in ragged formation. The boots and rifles and bayonets sticking in the ground. The ceremony of it, the reverence of the entire gathering. He couldn't hear the words; they were too far away for that. But if he had tried to edge in closer, he knew with gut instinct that he would be entering a cobra den. This was a conclave of grief that naturally shunned outsiders for their inability to share in it. So Private Nix watched, and Private Nix learned.

When the sergeant major gave the final word of dismissal,

and the Marines disbursed – to where Elmore didn't know – a hulk of a man approached, a battered cigar nub sticking out of his mouth.

He marched over like he could stomp out a mountain range. He looked them up and down.

"You the boots?"

It was the too-eager one, the kid from Tallahassee who answered.

"Yes, sir. Private—"

The sergeant shut him off with a glare. "I don't care what your name is right now, Marine. All I want to know is that you were assigned to this unit."

"Here are our orders, Sergeant," Elmore said, handing the Marine a stack of papers. The sergeant gave them a quick once-over, grunting intermittently.

"Who's Jasper, Brian K?"

"That's me, sir," said a weak voice.

"That's me, *Sergeant*."

Private Jasper righted himself. "That's me, Sergeant."

"Says here you're from Johnson City, Tennessee. That true?"

"Yes, Sergeant."

"Ever eat at The Peerless restaurant?"

Private Jasper perked up. "Yes, Sergeant! I used to go there every Sunday with my family."

Another glare from the old salt. "So you're just another momma's boy. Probably never worked a day in your life. Let me guess, you made it into town every Sunday, probably had a nice meal, and then headed over to the damn pharmacy for an ice cream soda."

Jasper went white. "Yes, Sergeant."

"Did you have sprinkles on your sundae, Private?"

"Chocolate sprinkles, Sergeant."

"Chocolate sprinkles."

The cigar shifted from one side of the sergeant's mouth to another.

"They never let my kind into town on Sundays, Jasper. But around here, I'm the boss, your holy father, the head man in charge of your life, however pitiful it might be. You got that?"

"Yes, Sergeant!" Private Jasper barked, now standing at full attention.

"And keep your goddamned voice down. You want every gook from here to Hanoi to know our location?"

Everyone looked around, as if expecting a morning raid at that very moment. Everyone except for the salty sergeant and Private Nix.

"What about you, mister? What's your name?"

"Nix, Sergeant."

"Nix. As in ixnay? Are you shitting me, boy?"

"No, Sergeant."

"What are you, some kind of used car salesman? Nix sounds like some sleazy salesman name. What'd you say, Nix, you gonna sell me an insurance policy? Or maybe a new vacuum?"

Nix suppressed a smile. He didn't know why he wanted to smile. Maybe it was the twinkle of amusement in the older Marine's eyes.

"No, Sergeant. I've never been in sales."

Their eyes stayed locked, Nix never backing down.

"Well, that's good, Nix. Very good. Cuz I wouldn't buy a hot dog for my starving grandma from you." Then the sergeant turned his attention back to the others.

"Listen up, ladies. My name's Franks, and I'm your mommy, daddy, preacher, and savior. You listen to me and I'll do my best to keep you alive. If you don't—well—I won't be responsible for stupidity."

CHAPTER TWENTY-EIGHT

The letters were gone by the time Sam arrived. She looked tired.

"Have a nap. You can take the guest room if you want," Elmore said. "Sheets are clean."

It was a new step in their relationship, and he thought he detected a cringe. Maybe not revulsion. No, more like... what was it? Carefulness with a sprinkling of caution, like tiptoeing into a Broadway show through the back door.

"I'm fine," Sam said, punctuating the 'fine' with a yawn.

Maybe that's how all teenagers were. Elmore didn't know. He couldn't remember. He'd forgotten more about his own teenage years than he remembered.

"So?" Sam asked, flopping down in an armchair, backpack falling to the floor.

"So what?"

A roll of the eyes. "You know what, Elmore Thaddeus Nix."

He grinned. It was impossible not to. To see her exasperated gave him a mischievous satisfaction. Perhaps he did remember what being a teenager was like after all.

"Why do you use my full name?"

"Are you kidding? If I had your name I'd say it out loud all day long."

"It's a terrible name."

Her face screwed up. "What?"

"It is. My mother thought it sounded grand, like a philosopher's name, though I doubt she knew the difference between Plato and Pluto."

Sam made a disgusted noise. "I won't go into your mommy issues, Elmore Thaddeus Nix, but I will tell you that being unique is something to be treasured, not tossed in the trashcan."

It sounded like something from a Hallmark card. Again he grinned. He couldn't help it.

She rose from her chair in mock indignation. "Oh, now you're laughing at me? Look at my name, Samantha Jane Smith. Could I be any more boring?"

"It's a fine name," he said.

"A fine name. That's like saying last place is okay because you tried hard. Come on, Samantha Jane Smith is about the most vanilla name my parents could've given me."

He found himself unable to stop laughing. It was Sam's influence, no doubt, but there was something else. Perhaps a flood of emotion from the letters.

The words came out before he could stop them. "I want you to come with me."

"Where?" she was still smiling.

"To the banquet, you freak."

The smile waned for the briefest instant, and then returned. "Serious?"

"You got me into this mess. So whad'ya say, Samantha Jane Smith? Will you be my date?"

CHAPTER TWENTY-NINE

The dinner, or banquet, or whatever it was, was held in the Embassy Suites in Chicago, a four-hour drive. Sam chatted the entire way. There'd been no issues with Sam's mom, at least none that Elmore could tell.

Rather than ask his old compatriots to foot the bill, he'd booked two rooms at the Embassy Suites. It was agreed that they'd say Sam was his granddaughter. Fewer questions that way. They were friends, but both understood the oddity of the relationship.

They arrived just after noon on Saturday. The valet offered to have their bags taken to their rooms. Elmore tipped the man a five and said they'd be fine. He only had a small carry on and Sam had her trusty backpack.

He was grabbing for the door to the lobby when he realized Sam wasn't with him. He turned and found her gazing straight up at the ceiling.

"Sam?"

She put a hand up to stall him. He waited, watching as she breathed in and out. Then with a long final inhale, she joined him.

"It's amazing, isn't it?"

"It is," he said. He didn't want to dampen her spirits by admitting that he hated the claustrophobia of being literally surrounded by concrete.

They'd worked out the logistics of their stay ahead of time. Since she was too young to stay in her own room, technically, Elmore did all the checking in while she waited near the fountain. Key cards now in hand, they proceeded to the bank of elevators.

He'd clammed up with each step, hoping he wouldn't run into any of his old friends. He wasn't yet ready for that.

"You okay?" Sam asked as the elevator doors shut.

"Just tired. Maybe I'll take a quick nap."

She looked disappointed, like she'd had other plans for them. But sightseeing was the last thing on Elmore's mind. His hands were wet. He rubbed his palms together, and then wiped them on his pants.

Then his hand was in hers. She didn't say a thing, didn't look at him. They just rose to the highest levels of the hotel, fake grandfather and granddaughter, hand in hand. It gave him strength. It kept him from running. But what would he do when she wasn't there?

CHAPTER THIRTY

He tried to sleep but couldn't, and so he got up and paced, watching the same swatch of carpet swish by before his eyes countless times. By the time five o'clock came, he was a nervous wreck. He showered, shaved, and put on his suit. It was his old trusty, the one he wore for baptisms and funerals. Every five years or so, Eve would buy him a new one, even though he could've kept the same. They didn't get much use.

But as he inspected himself in the mirror, he thought of her, the way she'd circle him, brushing lint from his sleeves, tightening his tie into place.

God, I miss you, he thought.

The knocking at the door jolted him from his wallow. It was Sam, exactly five minutes to five.

When he opened the door, he wasn't prepared for the vision.

She was wearing makeup, just enough. And her dress was light, appropriate for her age, and the entire effect made her positively glow.

"Wow, Sam."

She actually blushed. Then she regained her spunkiness and did a quick twirl. "Not bad, right?"

"You look fantastic," he said.

"And look at you, Elmore Thaddeus Nix. You sure clean up good. All set?"

"No, but I never will be. We'd better get downstairs before I chicken out."

She took his proffered arm, the young lady joining the ancient gentleman.

THE BALLROOM WAS spacious and packed. They approached a receiving table manned by a portly fellow with eyebrows that exploded over his eyes.

"Name?" he said without looking up.

"Nix."

The man looked up, a frozen expression on his face. "Sonofabitch. It's you."

Elmore read the name tag. "Gills."

It wasn't a chair the old Marine was sitting in. It was a wheelchair.

"If I could stand I would shake your hand, sir."

"A handshake will do just fine," Elmore said, offering his hand.

Gills took it and the stream of an old memory struck Elmore right in the middle of the eyes.

"Gills," he said, "as I recall, you were from Denver."

The bushy eyebrows waggled.

"That's right. Denver then, Tampa now. Got too cold for these old legs." He patted his meaty thighs, all that was left of him from the waist down. "Well look at me. Blubbering like I met my teen idol." He turned his attention to Sam, who was looking at her date with something akin to awe. "Now, young lady, you must be Corporal Nix's..."

"Granddaughter," she said without missing a beat. "Samantha."

"Like *Bewitched*," said Gills. "I had the biggest damn crush on that lady."

"You can just write Sam."

"Sam it is." He scribbled her name on a tag and handed it to her. "And for you, Corporal..." He snagged a tag sitting all by itself, professionally printed. "Did we spell it right?"

Corporal E.T. Nix.

Elmore had to swallow down the metallic taste in his mouth. He wanted nothing more than to flee, run home, and never come back.

But he pinned the tag to his lapel and tried to seem confident.

"It sure is an honor to see you again, Nix," Gills said. "And, Sam, if you happen to have a few minutes, and your granddaddy doesn't mind, I'd like to tell you a few stories I'm sure he's never told you."

"I would like that very much, Mr. Gills."

"What's this Mister? It's just Gills. Makes me feel like I'm back in the Corps."

They left the table as the memory wisp smacked Elmore in the back of the head. Pfc. Gills, screaming from just over the far hill. Pfc. Gills, probably seconds from dying. But it didn't matter. Lance Corporal Nix ignored his platoon commander. *Never leave a Marine to die*, he'd kept telling himself.

He made it to Gills, who was a bloody mess, one leg gone and the other hanging by a tether. Two hasty tourniquets later, and too many screams to count, he picked Gills up in a fireman's carry and ran the way he'd come.

God, he could still feel the weight in his legs. And yet he ran on, even as the enemy mortars that had taken out Gills' fire team rained down around them.

"Good Christ, look at what the cat dragged in!" The words shook Elmore back to the present. It was Franks, commanding a legion of his followers, just like in the old days. "And the lovely Sam. Young lady, you are the picture of classical beauty." He offered his hand and Sam took it without hesitation. "What are you doing on the arm of this war horse? Don't you know this guy doesn't need any help looking ugly?" Elmore smiled at her, beaming with pride for the girl. She no longer looked the part of a teenager. She looked like an escort to an emperor.

"And Nix, you sure clean up good."

"Right." Sam said, quite happy with herself.

There were handshakes all around. He'd caught sight of some of the guests ogling, too polite to come right out and pepper him with questions. Franks must have sensed the guest of honor's unease, because he ushered him to a table on the far side of the room.

"I saw the look on your face just now," Franks said. "Saw that look on a cow once. It was headed for the slaughterhouse."

"It's just a little surreal." Elmore said, looking all around the room. "I feel like someone reached into my head, yanked out a bunch of memories by the roots, and threw them down before me. I never thought I'd see any of these guys again."

"Hey," said Franks, "you know it doesn't matter how you feel about this stuff. These guys are here for you. It's what they're feeling. You understand?"

Elmore turned to his old friend. No, that wasn't right.

They'd never been friends. The Marine hierarchy wouldn't allow it. Their kinship was something deeper. A brotherhood bred in blood of the battlefield.

But for every positive emotion he had, there was a negative counterpart. This was about the damned medal again. He barely remembered it. Sure, he remembered the weary yet proud look of the president who'd pinned it on him. Sure, he remembered the trip to D.C. to receive it. But that trip had been important for other reasons, reasons that overshadowed what was supposedly a great honor.

"They're not here for me," Elmore said, wanting now more than before to leave. He'd said his hellos. Maybe he'd make one more pass and go.

Franks grabbed him by the shoulders and fixed him with a cold stare. "Listen. I don't know what you've been through, and I'm not rude enough to ask. But we've all been through a lot. You did your duty. I'm not asking you for a goddamned thing except to be here."

"Why? I just don't understand why."

Franks let go of his shoulders, took a deep breath in and motioned to the rest of the room. "Look around. What do you see?"

Elmore refused to show his cynicism to Franks. And so he wouldn't say that all he saw was a bunch of overweight and aging Marines and their families. "I don't know what I see," he said.

Tears came to Franks' eyes. "You stubborn bastard. We're here because of you, Nix. Every damned one of us."

No, Elmore thought. *That wasn't right. It couldn't be.*

Franks was looking at Sam now, tears streaming down his face. *My God, Franks is crying.* Talk about surreal.

"Your friend here, he saved us all that day. And not just

that day. Multiple times. This was the only one he got credit for. I've never seen a braver man than Corporal Elmore Thaddeus Nix."

The memories came back in full, bloody Technicolor...

CHAPTER THIRTY-ONE

The day started off like any other in the bush. Another patrol. Wet this day. The rains just kept coming. The day before had been dry and hot as Hades.

Elmore had a fire team now. The last fire team leader had been skewered by a Vietcong earlier in the week.

Up until then, now Lance Corporal Nix had just toed the line, kept his head down, listened, and watched the old timers. They were magnificent bastards, all. They jawed like hens, but when it came time to get to work, they just did it.

Nix's first firefight had been a night ambush. As the low man on the pole, he hadn't really known what was happening. Sure, there'd been the orders passed down, but by the time it got to him it was, "This is your spot. Keep your fire between this stick and this stick." He had his fire lane and that's all that mattered. Every boot Marine knew that the absolute worst sin a Marine could commit was fratricide; friendly fire. No one could live that down.

The ambush went off without a hitch. Five VC killed and Nix hadn't fired a single shot. He hadn't needed to, even though the men to his left and right all shot until their magazines were empty. When he asked them later what they'd shot at, the new Marines just said they thought they were supposed to fire when they heard the first shot fired.

Whittled down by attrition, he had four Marines, including himself. The heavy gun was his for the day. He liked the weight of it. But more than that, he loved its accuracy and raw power. When he lay down behind it, he felt like he'd been born with the weapon in his hands. No man in his platoon could wield the thing like he could. Even Sgt. Franks had grudgingly given him a pat on the back for his lethality behind the beast.

He was already an old salt by then. He felt like he'd aged like vintage bourbon, burning and perfect.

With the big gun, he still did his duty, toting the new kid behind him. He liked to keep the new ones close. Better to keep their jarred nerves in check. The new kid had the extra ammo. Piles of the stuff. If Nix asked for extra ammo it just appeared, scrounged from other platoons, battalions, or best yet, the Army.

This night was no exception, though he had the same feeling again that he'd had the first ambush. Something big was coming, like the soft hooves of a herd of cattle in the fields over the horizon. He could hear it. He psychically called to it.

Did that make it his fault?

Just after midnight, the rains returned, pounding this time. He didn't like to wear his poncho. It kept him from keeping a good grip on the big gun. He'd rigged a cut version that protected at least some of his body. The smell of wet vegetation was all around – pungent, sickening.

The new kid shivered behind him. He felt it. The strangest thing. How could he feel something like that? This country and its violence in the dark had heightened every one of his senses. When he looked back, the kid was staring at his feet, plodding along in a daze. Nix was about to tell him to look up, keep alert, but a line of tracers buzzed in and severed the new kid's head from his shoulders.

Chaos engulfed the platoon. Hasty positions. Hell itself had come to frolic on the surface of the earth.

Screams and the telltale sound of mortars *thunking* from tubes. The smell of burning metal and blood. Bits of stuff flying. Grains of dirt, blasted rocks, bone...

He was on the ground now, scanning for targets. Nothing. The screams of his companions went on like some sort of twisted opera.

That's when it all solidified and appeared like a map in his head. He saw it all. He knew that if he didn't do something, they'd all die.

So even as his squad leader was blown away and his platoon commander shouted for support over the radio, Lance Corporal Elmore Thaddeus Nix rose to his feet and took on the enemy.

CHAPTER THIRTY-TWO

"By *himself?*" said Sam.

Franks was staring at Elmore again. That damned look. *Why couldn't he look somewhere else? He was wrong, dammit.* This wasn't for him.

"He saved us all," Franks said. "They," and now he pointed to the families and old compatriots huddled around the tables, "they want to say thank you."

Elmore wiped his forehead. It was too hot in here. Someone was holding his hand. It was Sam. He looked down. She looked up.

There was a tapping of a microphone and all eyes turned to the podium.

"Ladies and gentlemen, if you'll all have a seat, dinner is about to be served."

Franks clapped Elmore on the back. "Come on. You're with me."

Elmore didn't taste the food. He barely registered the conversations going on around him. Instead, he was cast back once again, back to that night, back to the glory of it all.

How he'd fallen on the front line of the enemy like silent

death. How he noted the explosives wrapped around the body of a boy no older than thirteen.

Remember that, he'd told himself.

Tracers and mortars arced all around. The envelopment was coming. If the enemy made it all the way around, the Marines would be dead. Each and every one of them. It was in the lay of the land, the perfect kill zone. Fish in a barrel, as the saying went.

So, he killed, not because he liked to, not even because he wanted to, but because he had to. And because he was good at it.

HE MANAGED TO EAT EVERYTHING, despite his frayed nerves. He knew what was coming. He saw them staring, mothers pointing, children giggling as they wondered about the old man at the head table. *Whispers on the wind.* Or was that all in his head?

Franks rose, patted Elmore on the shoulder, and he marched to the podium. There were two generals in attendance — men Elmore had barely known at the time. Everyone knew the original salt, Sgt. Franks, was in charge.

The Marine took the stage with the relish they'd all admired, not an ounce of hesitation.

"Some of you may remember me as a younger, more gentile version of the crumbling marine standing in front you." There was polite laughter, rising to a near raucous when someone in the crowd piped in, "That's not what the ladies in Bangkok used to say."

Franks didn't color. He never did.

"Alright, settle down. Do I need to take you old coots out

back for some good old-fashioned chewing? And watch your mouths. There are children here."

But his face said it all. He loved the grand stage. He relished being surrounded by his Marines.

"Some of you I've kept up with over the years. Others, like you Sachowski, I can't seem to get rid of."

"That's right," Sachowski crowed. "You'll have to kill me first!"

Sachowski, Elmore thought. He was from... where? San Francisco? No. Sacramento. Funny how you remembered those things after all the years.

"Okay. Settle down or the general might have to call the commandant." Franks pulled a folded bill of notes from his pocket and set them on the podium. "Now, for the main event. We've been trying to do this for a long time. It's best we get it right the first time. So, if you'll excuse me, I'm going to refer to my notes." He pulled a pair of reading glasses from his shirt pocket. It was strange to see Sgt. Franks wearing glasses. It was like finding out that Superman was really Clark Kent — part mortal.

The crowd had gone silent, fully focused on the podium now, and on Elmore.

Franks coughed into the back of his hand. "First, I'd like to take a second to say thanks to all of you for coming. I know it wasn't easy, but we made it, didn't we? There were a lot of days when we thought we wouldn't make it. I've never forgotten, as I'm sure you haven't either. Sure, it's easy to say 'move on', but it's not easy. So, let's take a few moments to think of our friends who didn't make it, our friends who lost the battle with Father Time." Franks bowed his head and everyone followed suit. Elmore stared at his hands, wringing the napkin in his lap, trying to fight the rush of anxiety.

When the requisite time had passed, Franks looked up again. "Now, I promised you I wouldn't hog the stage."

"Go on and hog it, Sarge," Sachowski yelled.

Chuckles and a Cheshire grin from Franks.

"Alright, pipe down now, Marine. I've got a story to tell." Franks fussed with his notes, turning from one page to another. "Forget it." He crumpled the papers and tossed them to the ground. "Never good at writing anyway."

It took him a moment to gather his thoughts and then he settled into what Elmore thought of as the Franks stance, the same one he'd used before stepping off on patrol.

"I don't remember meeting then-Private Nix. All I recall is a truck full of fresh-cut Marines shows up and you try to block out how the new kids look like carbon copies of the Marines who just got carted off. I do remember how he used to shoot. You all remember. Nix could shoot the eyes off a pair of dice. A real natural." The MC gazed out over the crowd, fully immersed in the memory now. "It was some time during the rainy season that I realized he was made of different stuff. Yeah, I hear you groaning. I'll never forget the damned rainy season either. Anyway, I remember Nix on one of our endless patrols, never complaining. The lieutenant, God rest his soul, had put Nix on the radio. He was a sturdy young buck back then. Never complained. You remember that? Damnedest thing. All Marines complain, at least to their buddy in the foxhole. But not Nix. Nope. He lugged that radio up and down hills, kept it up and running, even though I'm pretty sure he only got a five-minute tutorial on how the thing worked.

"So there was the lieutenant, jabbering away, me nearby, and Nix looking into the bush. Out of nowhere, the VC attacked. They'd seen us coming. The lieutenant knew it, even though he'd been in country less than a month. God bless that baby-faced boy. He was the first to go. So what does Nix do? With the radio still on his back, he engages the enemy with focused, disciplined fire, just like in the manual. But that wasn't the beauty of it." Franks shook his head, as if the memory couldn't be right. "Pfc. Nix took a beat from firing, picked the lieutenant up onto his shoulder and moved toward the EVAC point. But you know what, he kept firing. Radio on his back. Officer on his shoulders, and still Nix fired. Damnedest thing..."

Elmore saw it. He felt it. He tasted the rain. He smelled the cordite, the blood of the young lieutenant running down his back. He hadn't thought. He'd just acted.

"Well, it wasn't the last time Nix would surprise me. No sir. That's why we're here, but now that I think about it, by the time he saved our tails it wasn't a surprise anymore. We knew Nix. He knew us. And we knew that we'd be okay as long as this special Marine stayed in our ranks. And that's where the story gets really interesting..."

CHAPTER THIRTY-THREE

They really were everywhere. VC for miles, for days.

He'd gotten lucky. They were focused forward, away from his approach. He'd somehow penetrated their hasty line and taken them on the flank. *Luck, pure luck*, he thought.

LCpl. Nix had the insight to know that he should keep the element of surprise. From position to position, he hopped, plunging his Ka-Bar into chest cavities, slicing necks and faces. Methodical. No trembling hands.

But the thirst was coming. Dull at first but coming for sure.

At some point, the enemy caught wind of what he was doing, and some of their forces turned. He didn't care. He was in no-man's land now, in the land of the enemy. Best to take it for what it was – an opportunity.

So he plodded on, doing his business. At least until the first artillery shells hit.

CHAPTER THIRTY-FOUR

"I'll never forget the sounds of those artillery rounds coming," Franks was saying. "Like freight trains. Sachowski, you remember, don't you? You were with me."

"Sure was, Sarge. Pissed my pants."

The Marines in the room laughed. The wives just smiled. They'd heard the stories over and over again.

"Artillery. Great when we're shooting at them, but never good coming in. So, there we were, in a real pickle. I call for Nix – I want his gun. But nobody can find him. He's gone, like so many others." Franks shifted his gaze to Elmore now. Elmore felt it, the tide turning straight at him. "So, that comes to you, my friend. I know you don't want to talk about it. I didn't for a long, long time. But my wife, Jenny, got me to a group and then to a professional." Franks took a deep breath in, let it out like it was the only thing keeping him alive. "There, I said it. I talked to a professional head-shrinker. Who wants to call me a mush brain for doing it? Folks, we've lost too many friends to the demons. Now we've got these wonderfully brave kids fighting in Iraq, Afghanistan, and they come home to a country that doesn't know what to do with them. At least they don't get the protests that we got. But still..." Franks shook his head. "Hell, I guess that's a story for another day. And I've said enough. I'll let these men talk for a bit."

That was when Elmore looked up and saw the line that had, at some point formed on the far side of the stage. It wrapped halfway around the room. What was happening?

Franks read his mind. He looked right at him when he said, "Nix, sit back. They're going to tell your story."

CHAPTER THIRTY-FIVE

"Corporal Nix carried me a hundred yards after tying my legs off," one old Marine in a wheelchair said, his smile as wide as the sunrise. His name was Lloyd and he spoke with a slight stutter. "I was fat then too, so I don't know how. The heat should've taken the weight from me, but there it is. Fat and bleeding to death, and here comes Nix, covered in blood and mud. I don't know why, but when he said I was gonna be okay, I believed him. Even months later, when the doctors said I had a ten percent chance of living. I told them that Nix said I'd be okay. They asked me who Nix was and I told them, and then I got back to healing."

Another Marine took the mic, a handsome, put-together, retired doctor type. "I'd run out of ammo and the VC were everywhere. I was about to fall back to find some ammo when all of a sudden, Nix hops into my foxhole with a fresh set of rounds. 'Take the shots you know you'll make,' he told me. And so I did. I took my time. Something about the way he told me – so calm, even over all the noise of the battle. I listened and I lived to fight another day."

Then there was the family, a woman and her son.

"There wasn't a day that went by that my husband didn't talk about Corporal Nix. Corporal Nix this and Corporal Nix that. I started to get sick of hearing the name."

Chuckles from the crowd.

Her son spoke. "When we were kids, Pops always came home in time to say our prayers with us. The first person we'd thank God for was Corporal Nix. We didn't know who he was. We thought he was an angel. I guess to Pops, he was."

The general stepped up next and looked out over the crowd, this probably his thousandth performance. His eyes locked like an eagle's, completely focused and still looking like he could do pull-ups with a pack on even though he had to be well into his seventies. "For those of you who don't know, I had the privilege of being the company commander for this rag tag bunch of Marines. We were told to distance ourselves emotionally, for we were sure to lose a lot of men. That was Vietnam. I saw the body bags loading the day I arrived. Helluva way for a twenty-something kid to be initiated. But these Marines, these wonderful bastards, well, they showed me what life was really like. They showed me that you could have the foulest mouth in the China Sea, but that compassion was at the heart of every man." He turned to Elmore, his gaze piercing. Elmore wanted to turn from it. "And then there was Nix. Elmore Thaddeus Nix. A man as uncommon as his name. Like Sergeant Franks, I don't remember the day he arrived. There were too many other things to think about. I was a good Marine and I distanced myself. But things changed, not just on that fateful night, but every day after Nix came to Vietnam. Now, I'm not gonna sit up here and preach to you, but I do believe, I truly do, that even in the midst of a godforsaken war, God is still watching. He's watching, waiting, and every once in a while, he sends us a blessing in the form of another man or woman. I've had the privilege of serving with too many good Marines to count, but when I think of the pinnacle of God's gift, my mind always goes to Corporal Nix. You were God's gift to every man, woman, and child in this room, and I thank you."

It went on like that for the better part of two hours. Elmore squirmed through it all. These memories came to him at the oddest times over the years. Blessed memories of war and blood and the men he'd served with.

And then there was *the* memory.

The one that never went away.

CHAPTER THIRTY-SIX

The day after the battle, everyone back at headquarters seemed to be talking. They were in the process of debriefing the Marines, top down. There was talk of a new offensive, something to capitalize on the route of a VC regiment spearheaded by a single Marine company. That's what it had turned into.

But LCpl. Nix wasn't thinking on that now. He'd found a place on a hill overlooking the landscape of green. A stack of cigarette packs sat next to him. He puffed away, not quite knowing what to think, but he knew what he felt: pride. Sinful, yes, but pride nonetheless. The pride of a man who never really knew his purpose on earth and suddenly did. The pride of a man who'd been trained for a single task and had come through it clean.

And so he sat, and he smoked, and he thought. He'd finally come to the place in his life when he knew he'd made it. He'd become the thing he most admired, and it made him smile.

LCpl. Elmore Thaddeus Nix had done his best, and his best had been enough.

His mind went down the dove trail of future plans and he saw himself as a gunny, maybe even a first sergeant one day. Yes, that would be worthwhile. He'd volunteer to stay past his time. The jungles of Vietnam had shown him his worth, and he meant to spend that worth until the day he could no longer raise a weapon to defend his friends – his brothers.

But fate had another plan, and it would be weeks until LCpl. Nix found out that his own plans had been discarded like so much obsolete refuse.

CHAPTER THIRTY-SEVEN

Sam had taken Elmore's hand again and clutched it fiercely. So strange, that feeling.

Sgt. Franks was at the podium again. "Nix, I hope you have a better understanding of why we've spent the last twenty years inviting you to this thing. We just wanted to say thanks. Truly. Deeply. Thank you." The notes came out again but went away just as fast. "Who was there when they pinned the medal on Nix?"

A scattering of raised hands.

"I wish I could've been there," Franks said, wistful now. "General, is it true that Nix tried to give it back?"

The general nodded reverently.

Franks smiled. "It was probably the one and only time Nix disobeyed a direct order."

And it was. He'd stepped right up to the commanding general and offered to give the medal back. He didn't want it. Everything they'd said in the citation, about fighting nonstop for two days and saving all those Marines, was all true. But it was the burden that came along with it that Elmore didn't want.

CHAPTER THIRTY-EIGHT

Now-Corporal Nix entered the battalion hooch, wiping the sweat from his brow, just off another of a long line of patrols. It wasn't just the colonel there. A chaplain was there too, along with three generals. One looked like he'd been in the country. The other two had the look of someone fresh off the plane, though by the look in their eyes and the way they didn't flinch at the sound of artillery, he knew they'd seen combat in their prime.

He reported in like he'd learned at Parris Island. "Corporal Nix reporting as ordered, gentlemen."

He'd said 'gentlemen' at the last moment. Was that what he was supposed to say in the company of all those stars?

"At ease, Nix," the regimental commander said. Nix had limited contact with the man. For all he knew, the colonel was a fair but tough man — a man who knew the business of war. "The general's here to deliver your orders."

There were smiles all around.

"I'm sorry, sir?"

"Your orders, Nix. You're going home."

"That can't be right. I've got two months left, sir."

The colonel walked over and clapped Nix on the back. "Not anymore you don't. It's come straight from the president. He wants to see you and put the medal around your neck himself."

"But—"

"You don't want to go home, do you, Nix?" He looked at the other generals. "The crazy sonofabitch wants to stay."

The generals laughed. The chaplain stared at his feet, a smile playing around his lips.

Now the colonel's face went hard. "Look, son, you've done good. But you're no good to me here. I can't have the burden of a Medal of Honor recipient under my command. Hell, what would happen if you got killed?"

Nix couldn't believe what he was hearing.

"Then I don't want it, sir. I don't want the medal."

This time the colonel's tone said it all. "It's done, son," was all he said.

And so that was it. The choice was final, and there wasn't a thing Cpl. Nix, meritoriously promoted or not, medal or not, could do about it.

"Is there anything I can do to stay, sir?"

"Not a damn thing, Marine. And as of this very second, you will not go outside the wire. Understood?"

And just like that, Cpl. Nix never raised a weapon in battle again.

CHAPTER THIRTY-NINE

"There are many more stories we'll never hear, stories our friends took to the tavern in the sky. We'll hear them again, some of us sooner than others." Franks turned back to Elmore. "Thank you for coming, Nix. Thank you for letting us say thank you. You saved one hundred and seventy-four men that day and who knows how many men, women, and children on the other days. By our crude estimates, your actions not only saved the lives of one hundred and seventy-four men, but you allowed us to grow to more than five hundred with our wives and children and our children's children. I hope you understand that we are part of your legacy. It can never be undone. And even though the generations that come after us might not know your name, Elmore Thaddeus Nix, that name will be forever etched on their being."

There was a raucous round of clapping, men and women taking to their feet. All for him. The man who had lost it all. Twice.

An hour before, he might've run. He'd thought about excusing himself to go to the bathroom and then slipping out the back door to safety.

Now, something else grabbed him, pulled him to his feet even as the others took their seats again. There hadn't been a request for him to speak. Franks knew better. They all knew better. It had been what felt like eons since Vietnam, but he was still Elmore Nix – a man of few words.

Franks stepped down from his perch whispered in Elmore's ear, "You don't have to, you know."

"I want to."

An all-encompassing smile took over the face of the indomitable Sgt. Franks. "It's yours for as long as you like." He waved to the stage, and Elmore found himself taking sure steps to the spotlight.

CHAPTER FORTY

"My Eve would've liked this," he said, his smile coming naturally. "She would've liked all of you. You see, I never told her about Vietnam. Not a single story, if you can believe that. I always thought it was bad form for a Marine to talk about his experiences to civilians. My wife didn't marry a killer. And so, how could I tell her that I had killed? Oh, she was a smart cookie, don't get me wrong. She knew what Marines did in times of war. But I always felt that she wouldn't look at me the same way if I had actually told her about it. Only a fellow Marine or soldier can understand that, and so I have no trouble telling any of you this. But I came home feeling terrible, and not necessarily for what I'd had to do. I always felt like I left before my time was up, like I cheated somehow. Some general shows up and gives me the golden ticket home. I'm babbling here, I guess, and I apologize.

"The other reason I shut up about my experiences was because I was selfish. I wanted to keep you all to myself. Because, you see, you were part of the first great chapter of my life. You were there. My life was yours and yours mine. Other than a marriage, I don't know if there's a deeper connection than the one between men, and now women as well, fighting in a war a million miles from home." His gaze scanned the crowd. Tears. Nods of reassurance. Snifflings into a napkins. "War is hell because of death. No one wants to die. I didn't. You didn't either. But in that uncertainty, something funny happens. It happened to me. I went from boy to man. I gained an understanding of myself that I never could've received anywhere else. It was the best school, the best stepping stone..."

He shook his head. *Where was he going with his babble?*

"I haven't given much time to God lately. That's on me. I'm angry, and I might be for some time. That's okay. He'll be there when I'm ready. I truly believe that. It was my wife, Eve, who taught me of God's love. I only wish I told her about you."

The tears were coming now. *God, how he missed her.* He wanted to walk from table to table with her holding onto his arm, taking time to introduce her to every face, every name. Tell her the stories. Let her glow in what might possibly be his best accomplishment, the jewel of his early years.

Eve, give me the strength...

"Ah, I don't know what the hell I'm saying. The last thing I want to do is waste your time."

"Waste it all you want!" Sachowski crowed, raising his cocktail glass in the air.

There were murmurs of approval. Cheers to continue.

But he didn't know if he could. His vision was going fuzzy now from tears.

"I'm grateful for the invitation, for this time with you. I promise..." Lord, it was getting hot up here. "I won't be a stranger. I..."

What was I saying? And did I just think that or did I say it?

They were blurs now, shimmering and dark around the edges.

Why was the crowd rushing toward him like the tide?

CHAPTER FORTY-ONE

The beep and whir were there again. He knew the sound before he opened his eyes.

My, he'd had a wonderful dream. Eve had been right there in Vietnam with him. It was after the war, what it probably looked like now – fresh and lush with all manner of deep green. But they were young again. They'd taken a boat, a small dingy from some unseen ship. His old Marines buddies were there to greet them, introducing themselves one by one to his wife. And like she'd always done, she gave them that special part of her, the way she made everyone feel like the most important person in the room at that point in time. She'd stop time for you.

He wanted to go back. He tried to push the new sounds away.

"Elmore Thaddeus Nix," came the whisper.

He couldn't ignore that as much as he wanted to. The voice sounded thin and scared. He had to go to it.

"Sam?" he was just able to croak as he blinked back to the present.

"I'm here," she said.

"Let me guess, I passed out again. Should've had more water."

Sam sniffed. How long had she been crying? Why had he put her through this again? This was nothing for a teenager to see.

"You weren't dehydrated. It was the tumor."

The damned word sent a chill through his body.

"The tumor," he echoed.

"Why didn't you tell me?"

"I did."

"You didn't tell me how bad it was."

"I can't believe the doctors told you. I'm gonna have a word with them." He slipped his legs out from the sheets, meaning to give his old friend the doc a good tongue-lashing.

Sam held him down. "Chill out. They didn't tell me. I heard them talking."

So stupid, he thought. It reminded him of those medical shows Eve liked to watch. She'd also talk about how naïve it was for hospital staff to talk in a hallway or in a place they were bound to be overheard.

"Sam, don't worry about it. I'm fine."

"You're not fine." There was anger in her tone. "Mr. Franks came with the ambulance. They wouldn't let me. I didn't know if..." She broke away, her face scrunching into childlike sadness.

She thought I died.

He reached out with his IV-tethered hand and grasped hers.

"I'm here, Sam. I'm going to be okay."

She shook her head over and over again, finally looking up through bloodshot eyes and streaming tears. "How can you say that? You knew and you didn't tell me. And you didn't do a thing."

"Sam, it's more complicated..."

"You want to die, is that it? You don't care anymore. You lost your wife so now you think that killing yourself is the way to see her again."

He wanted to tell her it wasn't true, but how could he lie? He wanted to be with his Eve more than anything. He wanted to hold her, smother her in his embrace, smell her hair, touch the curve of her back, and inhale her loveliness. Even on her death bed, she'd been his angel.

But he couldn't go yet. He couldn't leave Sam to face her pain alone. How could he? He wasn't that cruel.

Then again. He had been that cruel. He'd turned a blind eye. He'd turned his back once before.

"Call the doctor, Sam."

Sam looked at him, a fair helping of suspicion there, like he was going to ask for a vial of strychnine. "Why?"

He tried to force a smile, but it hurt. "I'm going to do it."

"Do what?"

"I'm going to get better."

CHAPTER FORTY-TWO

The oncologist was thorough, with enough empathy to show that she cared, but just enough standoffishness to show that she'd done this hundreds, if not thousands of times – and to prove that emotion would not get in the way of the task at hand.

"So, we start tomorrow, Mr. Nix."

Elmore nodded and patted Sam's leg. It was unorthodox to have non-kin with you, but nobody batted an eye. Sam wouldn't let him go alone.

"Is there anything else we should know?" Sam asked, very much playing the motherly roll. She'd even found a pad of paper and hadn't stopped jotting down notes.

"Your granddaughter's on top of this," the doctor said.

"She got all the brains in the family," Elmore said.

"Good to know. Well then, to be clear, we've lost time."

"It's okay," Sam said, not looking up. "He'll be fine."

The doctor knew better than to correct a teenager, but she and Elmore shared a look. Elmore understood. His chances weren't the best. At least he had a chance and he meant to take that chance, if not for himself, then for Sam.

"Okay then. I'll see you after your first round of therapy."

There were handshakes all around. No hugs.

No doctor hugs a man headed for the slab.

THEY GOT lunch at McDonald's even though Sam protested.

"You should be eating healthy – salads, maybe some pasta."

"I want a burger, fries, and a shake." There was no stopping this one. Sam acquiesced and ordered a couple of burgers for herself.

When they got to his house, it was nearing dusk. He realized she hadn't left his side for three days, not even for a change of clothing.

"Sam, I'm stupid for not asking earlier, but does your mom know where you've been?"

No hesitation. "Of course."

They pulled into the garage, the old door squeaking its ancient hello.

"Why don't I give you a ride home?"

"I'm fine. I like walking." She was quick to answer. Too quick.

"Sam, it's almost dark. Why don't..." his hand was already going to shift the car into reverse. She reached up and grabbed it.

"I said I'm fine."

No sense arguing. If there was anything he knew about Sam, it was that arguing tended to get him to one place: right where she wanted.

"Okay."

She surprised him then. "Maybe you're right. Is it okay if I stay in the guest room?"

MORNING CAME after Elmore's third trip to the bathroom. He was still purging the excess fluids they'd pumped into him at the hospital. Even over the toilet flushing, he still heard the banging at the front door, followed by the incessant ringing of the doorbell.

He shuffled down the hall, catching Sam's head peaking blearily out of the guest room.

"Everything okay?" she asked, her hair matted to one side of her head.

"Just fine. Go back to bed."

It wasn't seven o'clock yet. Who in the world could it be?

He opened the door mid-knock, causing the woman who'd been doing the pounding to hop back in surprise, arm still extended.

She was wearing what looked like week-old makeup, caked on the eyes and rosy on the cheeks. It was the weathered look of someone who'd worked a hundred too many graveyard shifts, with the wary eyes of a kicked cat.

"May I help you?" Elmore asked, thinking for sure that she had the wrong house. He searched her face for some recognition that he knew her.

"You've got my daughter." Her words slashed out like a whip.

"I'm sorry?"

"My daughter, Samantha. I know she's here."

A cell phone came out like a pistol, poised and ready. "I've got the cops on speed dial, you old perv. I don't know who the hell you are, but you're going to give me my damn daughter."

"Ma'am, if you'd like—"

"What I'd like is for you to get my daughter and leave her the hell alone."

The phone was raised higher now, as if he needed the added threat.

He was stuck between a bewildered state of shock and mild anger.

"I'll be right back. Can I get you a cup of—?"

"Just get my daughter." Sam's mother placed her foot inside the door, just to make sure he wouldn't lock her out.

He made his way down the hall, wondering how he was going to wake Sam up, tell her what was happening. But there she was, her backpack in hand, brushing away the strands of hair from her face.

"It's my mom, isn't it?"

"It is."

She looked down at her feet, then back up at Elmore. "I'm sorry."

"You don't have to be sorry, Sam, but I thought she—"

"She's not well."

He held back any further judgment on the woman's appearance. "At least she knew where to find you."

"She tracked me." Sam fished out her phone. It took a long moment for his non-tech brain to register. You could track phones now. That wasn't just a domain for the CIA or the FBI anymore. Mothers and fathers could track the whereabouts of family members.

But Sam had said she couldn't afford the bill and that the phone didn't work in the traditional sense. That's what she'd said.

"I should go."

He stepped in her way, wanting to protect her for some reason. His senses were up now. Something about the mother. Something about the way Sam seemed to crumble and bend toward the woman in the doorway. This wasn't the confident girl he'd come to know. This was someone else, a girl who'd been put in her place.

"Maybe we should have some breakfast. I can invite your mom in. I can make pancakes."

"She doesn't eat breakfast," Sam said.

And that was that.

He escorted her to the door, making the transfer without a word.

"Talk to my daughter again and you're going to jail."

Little did she know that he had nothing left to lose, of course, except Sam.

CHAPTER FORTY-THREE

One day. Two days. Three.

Still no Sam.

Elmore had no way of getting in touch with her, not having her address or number. He tried going about his day avoiding any thought of her. The efforts were in vain. His thoughts were always with Sam.

On the third day, a visit from Sgt. Franks broke up the monotony of constant concern. They sat in the kitchen and threw small talk over cups of black coffee.

"What brings you around?"

"I was in the neighborhood," said Franks.

"Is that so?"

The old soldier smiled. "Alright, I'm checking up on you. Shoot me."

"I don't need a babysitter."

"Are you going to treatment?"

"I've got an appointment tomorrow," Elmore said, pouring a second cup for his old friend.

"Sam in school?"

"Yep," said Elmore, taking a noisy slurp from his mug.

"Nice girl. I sure like her. What grade she in again?"

"Sophomore."

"She coming by later?"

What was with the grilling? "Don't know."

"Huh." Franks sipped his coffee in deep thought, then said, "You know, you were so popular that the guys want to have another dinner, planned post haste."

"Yeah, well, they may have to wait a bit for that."

"Uh huh. Oh, you'll like this," said Franks. "That night at the banquet, I had to stop and put on my glasses in order to read my speech. I heard some murmurs in the crowd – jokes at my expense. I didn't care, of course. Anyway, afterward, I thought about it. It reminded me of a story I'd heard once about George Washington. Would you like to hear it?"

"Sure."

"Well, at the tail end of the war, the old man had to address a session of Congress. He took out his speech and paused to put on his glasses. 'Gentlemen,' he said, 'you will permit me to put on my spectacles, for, I have grown not only gray, but almost blind in the service of my country.' It was a very subtle way of reminding people of how long he'd served, and without pay, mind you."

Elmore smiled at this.

"Not bad, eh?"

"It's a good one."

"We're all older now, Nix. We served and we have that behind us. It's something to hold onto. Meaning. That's all. There's nothing deeper in it than that."

Elmore let that thought sink in as the two men sipped in relative silence.

THE DAY of his first treatment came. Afternoon and still no Sam.

After a brief spell of procrastination in the car, his leaden legs took him through the parking lot and into the building. It took a couple wrong turns before he found the right office. And there, standing in front of the waiting room door, was Sam.

"You're early," she said by way of greeting.

He had the overwhelming urge to hug her. "I am," he said instead.

Then they slipped into their old routine as if nothing had happened. No mom pounding on the door. No cancer. Just them.

The sticks and tubes weren't bad. Sam stayed with him the whole time, jabbering on about this school project and that schoolyard rumor. She was trying to distract him. He was glad for it. If someone had put a gun to his head, he might've admitted that he was afraid. Terrified. He managed to hide it well. He always did. He had when the doctor told Eve and him about Eve's diagnosis. He had when well-wishers came to her wake.

That fear, he thought, *when does it go away?*

Never, he realized. It only gets shrunk to a size that you can deal with.

The treatment was altogether pretty darned smooth. The mood was somber at times, melancholy when the woman next to him staggered to her feet, looking as emaciated as a prison camp survivor. But there was Sam, quick to help her. She smiled in return. It was an Eve moment.

The afternoon ended too quickly. Sam said her goodbye in the parking lot.

"You sure you don't want to grab a bite to eat?"

"Elmore Thaddeus Nix, I'll be in touch soon."

He didn't like the sound of that declaration.

"I don't have your phone number," he said.

Sam cocked her head to one side and pursed her lips. She'd told him that her phone didn't work in the traditional sense, but he knew better now. The mom tracking thing.

She rustled through her backpack to find a piece of paper and scribbled her cell phone number down, capped off with a little smiley face.

"I'll call you," he said.

"Nuh uh. Text me."

He wasn't much of a texter and was thoroughly unschooled in how to do it. But he nodded anyway. He wouldn't be using the number to text anyway.

Sam didn't know that as she walked away. He watched her until she was lost in the crowd of cars.

CHAPTER FORTY-FOUR

Elmore put the phone back in its cradle with a grunt. He was not a man without connections, but even his contacts had come up empty-handed. He wanted to know where Sam lived, if only to do a drive-by and see if she was okay.

It had been four days since seeing her. He was worried, more so with each passing day.

There was one last call to make. One last favor he could call in.

"John, it's Elmore. I need a favor."

HE SAT IN HIS CAR, two blocks away from the rundown motel parking lot. He'd been there for twenty-four minutes, and in that time observed three drug transactions. It was a slick affair. A car would pull into a space marked with a cone. Then a woman in a slinky outfit came out of a room and spoke to the man or woman driving the car.

No money exchanged hands. Directions were given and

the car disappeared for a moment, then reappeared behind the motel, where another girl in equally revealing wear took the money and delivered the goods.

This second woman he recognized as Sam's mother.

Elmore stewed over the problem. It would be easy to pull into the marked spot and pretend he was a buyer. But then what? It was just as likely that the police might show up. How stupid would it look if he got arrested? How would that help Sam?

And so he sat. An hour went by. Then another. No Sam. Just drug deals.

He was getting hungry and had to go to the bathroom. Then the unavoidable happened. The downside of his treatment. He had to drive away for a few minutes to find a place to vomit. He returned minutes later, lightheaded and covered in sweat.

I've missed her, I just know it, he thought, wiping his brow with a handkerchief he kept in his back pocket.

He was just getting ready to stomp his way across the street when he heard the sound of a bus from behind. Turning in his seat, he saw an elderly couple walk onto the bus stop concrete, and then there she was – Sam.

She had the seasoned look of a pro, glancing this way and that, collar pulled up just so.

What now, Elmore?

His paternal instincts took over. The same instincts that had saved his Marines. He started the car and did a quick U-turn, cursing to himself at the squeal of tires. More than one onlooker looked up from whatever it was they were doing. He was sure more than one motel blind was peeled open to see what the disturbance was.

Sam saw it too.

"Get in the car," he said, passenger side window down, engine running.

"Elmore...?"

"Get in the car, Sam."

She glanced at the motel then back to him. He thought she was going to protest. He saw the conflict in her eyes.

"Please, Sam," he said, more gently this time.

Like a prisoner who'd finally found her salvation, Sam opened the car door and shrank into the seat. She didn't buckle her seatbelt and Elmore didn't care. He wanted her as far away from the cursed place as he could get.

CHAPTER FORTY-FIVE

The crying started a mile away. He figured it must be the gravity of the situation. Or maybe she'd had a bad day. He didn't want to pry. She'd tell him in time, or at least he hoped she would.

"Hungry?" he asked when her silent tears subsided.

Sam shook her head.

They drove on, Elmore thinking.

"Where do you want to go?" he asked at one particularly long red light.

"Can we go for a walk?"

"Of course."

"At our park."

He grunted and made a U-turn, red light be damned.

The park was littered with children riding bikes and men and women in various forms of circuitous exercise. As soon as they got out of the car, Elmore could feel his young companion relax. He stepped onto the concrete path that meandered through the trees and over shallow hills. Sam looked up, closed her eyes, and sighed.

Elmore waited until her eyes opened and she looked at him.

"Okay. I'm ready."

As they made their way around the first turn, barely registering the activity all around them, Sam told her story.

SHE WALKED SLOWLY as she talked, parsing her words along with the rhythm of their feet on the pavement.

"No kid really wants to be free," she said. "I'd hear other kids talk about their parents – how strict they were. I would've killed for that kind of strictness. Don't get me wrong, it was nice staying up as late as I wanted and eating all kinds of junk. But I didn't enjoy the sounds of my mom getting it on with one nameless man after another in the other room. I grew up fast, you know?

"We were on assistance. I came to school one time too many without lunch and someone noticed. They gave this form for mom to fill out. I didn't want her to, so I did. They gave me a card and from then on, I got my lunch. I got made fun of. My card looked different from everyone else's. Why do you suppose they do that? I mean, don't they know kids have enough to deal with?

"We moved about ten times, and each move was worse than the last one. The last place was this never-ending freak show. Strangers in and out of the place. No one ever bathed. It was really gross. I kept to my room and read magazines. In the morning I'd go into the kitchen and find coke residue all over the table. And then, there was money. A lot of it. Mom was dealing."

She'd broken off, lost in trails of thought and memory.

"I don't like going home," she said after a moment.

Elmore understood. He felt pain radiating off the strong young woman. He didn't want to ask, but he had to. He had to know.

"Did she ever... did any of them ever hurt you?"

Sam didn't look up.

"My mom hits me sometimes. She's not very strong, but it hurts. I've learned when she's mad to just stay away. It's the... the others that really hurt. To this day I don't know if they were boyfriends or customers."

Elmore's heart broke for the girl. Cancer was nothing compared to what this child had been through. Why wasn't there a quiet island for discarded children to live out their lives in peace, free of the pain of broken adulthood?

A question ate away at his insides.

"How did they hurt you, Sam?"

Still she didn't look up. She licked her lips. Her mouth sounded sticky and parched.

"I don't want to talk about it, okay?"

Every inch of Elmore's body trembled. He felt his fists clenching involuntarily, his jaw clamping.

"I'm alright, Nix," Sam said.

He wanted to tell her that she wasn't okay, that what had happened to her wasn't okay. Decent parents didn't do that to children.

Then he stopped. He remembered. *Hypocrite*, he said to himself.

"Can I tell you a story?" he said.

Sam nodded, picking up an errant dodge ball and tossing it back to a group of youngsters.

Elmore pushed down his disgust for what he'd heard. It was no use at this juncture. No. He had to tell her. She thought he was some sort of saint. A cancer-ridden, weak-jointed saint.

"I have a son," he said, finally.

Now she looked up.

"You said your wife couldn't have children."

Elmore nodded gravely, the pain of what he was about to say bubbling through his laboring lungs.

"That is what I said. But I do have a son."

"How?"

"We adopted."

"Oh. You said *had?*"

The flashes of memory almost made him stop walking. He thought he was going to faint. It took a few breaths before he could explain.

"That's what I said. And no, he didn't die." *Now or never*, he thought. "I did a bad thing, Sam."

CHAPTER FORTY-SIX

They sat themselves down on a bench and watched park-goers. Sam sat with her hands folded in her lap, as still as he'd ever seen her. She looked like she was in church.

Finally, he began. "We adopted a healthy baby boy. A teenage mother had given him up. He had these blue eyes. Deep blue. You never saw blue like this. Eyes as blue as the ocean. It was the happiest Eve had ever been." He paused to wipe a tear from the corner of his eye and chuckled. "Look at me misting up now. I'm telling you, Sam, you should've seen her. She was a natural. She knew exactly what to do, from the diapers to the bottles. What a pro, my Eve."

"They say having a child changes you. For years, I thought that had to do with biology – that it only happened with the woman, and it couldn't happen with an adoption anyway. But that child changed me."

"What did you name him?" said Sam, staring straight ahead.

Anxiety roiled in his gut. He hadn't uttered the name in years. What power it held over him still. "Oliver," he said weakly.

Sam nodded her head. "Oliver Nix. Has a nice ring to it."

"We joined a social group for parents and adopted children. There were potlucks and game nights. Sometimes we'd take a trip to the aquarium. There was always a holiday party. The idea was to get the kids used to hearing the word adoption and having them associate it with this community of good people and fun times. We were always open about it. And so... Oliver... grew into an understanding of what it means to be adopted. There wasn't any one specific time that I can remember when we sat him down and told him the truth. We lived the truth. He was our son. Adopted was just a word."

"Oliver grew into a smart boy. Talented in sports, art, drama. Never got anything less than a B+ in school. In turn, we lumped our love onto him."

"Sounds like a good kid," said Sam.

Elmore smiled. "He was."

He wanted the story to end there.

"Tell me what happened," Sam said plainly. She sounded like Eve, that combination of compassion and no-nonsense steadfastness.

"I don't do well with change," Elmore said, rubbing the back of his hand absently. "You know me by now, Sam. You know that."

She nodded as he went on, firmly stuck in the flow of his story.

"He'd gone off to college. University of Chicago. It was when he came home for winter break that there was a disagreement, a rare thing in our family. Oliver wound up storming out of the house. Eve wanted me to go after him but I said that boys just need time to cool off. He stayed with a friend that night and went back up to school the next day

without saying goodbye. He sent for his things. After that...
well, that was it."

"What was it about?"

"The argument? I don't remember how it started. Politics,
probably. We never saw eye to eye on that. But we debated
each other fairly. I guess it just escalated that night. I just
didn't know how to give him what he wanted."

"I don't get it. What did he want?"

Elmore looked up to the fountain in the center of the
park, as if his son were about to emerge from it and answer
the question himself.

He exhaled, remembering the pain like a lasting wound to
the chest.

"I didn't understand, that's all. He wanted me to
understand."

"Understand what?"

Now his eyes drifted to Sam.

"I loved my son very much, Sam. So much that it still
hurts to think about it." His eyes went back to the fountain,
imagining the last image he'd ever had of his son. It wasn't
the anger or even the storming out of the house. It was the
look. At that moment, his son was alone, and it showed on
the boy's face. Then he was gone, never to return.

"Sam," he said after the image threatened to undo him
completely, "I didn't give Oliver a chance to show me who he
really was."

CHAPTER FORTY-SEVEN

They just sat there for a long while. Elmore imagining, Sam just waiting.

The sun went down before they moved. It was the growl of Sam's stomach that did it, shook Elmore from his trance.

"Will you look at me, staring off into space? I'm sorry, Sam."

"It's okay."

Elmore shook his head, getting to his feet.

"Let's go back home and I'll get us some dinner cooked up."

"Can I help?"

He looked at her and smiled. "More than you realize."

SAM DID ALL the talking as they chopped and scooped their way to the dinner table. No questions about Elmore's son. Nothing about Sam's mother. Mundane topics. The latest rumors at school. A funny thing she'd seen on YouTube.

Elmore relished it; he'd missed this kind of lightness in his life.

When they'd gotten their fill, pushed back from the dinner table, Elmore knew there was no getting around it. "What do you want me to do about your mother, Sam?"

She pursed her lips in thought. "It's a funny thing, family. Don't you think?"

"I guess it is."

"Right? As a kid, you assume your parents love you, and you love your parents, no matter what. Yeah, I'm like a teenager? And teenagers are supposed to be like all antsy and on the cusp of adulthood? But really we're just kids."

Sam was a walking contradiction. Here was the child out of the skin of the adult-before-her-time that he saw at the banquet.

"My mom's not a bad person, deep down. At least that's what I think. She's never been to treatment, and I don't think she'd ever go. Sorry, I'm just thinking out loud now."

"It's okay."

She was trying to be so strong, but Elmore saw the sadness there.

"But... like..."

"Just say it, Sam."

Tears welled in her eyes. She couldn't look at him. "I'm ashamed."

"It's not your fault."

"I know. I really do. But she's still my mother."

"That doesn't excuse what she's done."

That thought hung in the air for a long time.

"I don't want to go back."

The finality of the statement moved something in Elmore. He wanted to protect her, but until that moment, he hadn't been given the authority. Like a witness asking to be put in protection, Sam had just bequeathed her safety to Elmore.

"We'll take on life... together."

Sam nodded, tried to smile.

Then she asked something Elmore never expected.

"Can I help you find your son, too?"

CHAPTER FORTY-EIGHT

One night turned to two. Elmore plotted, made some calls while Sam hunkered down. It was a good thing it was the weekend, or there'd be school to contend with. It wasn't like it was in Elmore's days. Truancy was a serious matter now. Monday would be another story. Sam would either have to go to school, a place easily tracked by her mother and the school district, or they could come up with a plan.

"I need to run to the store," Elmore said, frustrated. They were no closer to a solution. Sam's mother probably needed to be arrested and put in treatment but Sam would have none of it. There was still that shred of love there, despite everything her mother had put her through. It still made Elmore nauseous just to think of it. The sick denting of her emotions that messed with her sense of loyalty.

"I can come with you," Sam offered.

"No, why don't you stay here."

Sam rolled her eyes. "Whatever. I guess I should stay and do the dishes. It *is* my turn."

Elmore would've been happy to have her come along on any other day, but today he had an extra errand to run.

HE WAS BACK in less than an hour, groceries in two bags, enough for two breakfasts, three lunches and a pair of dinners.

His first indication that something was off was that the front door left ajar. He'd locked it. He always did.

Maybe Sam went for a walk, he told himself. But she would've locked, or at least closed, the door.

As he got closer to the front of his house, he saw the crack in the doorframe. The grocery bags fell to the ground as he rushed forward, pushing his way through the door without a thought.

There was Sam, sitting on the couch, hands in her lap. But she wasn't alone. Her mother was sitting next to her, holding a cigarette in one hand, the thin line of smoke trailing up to the ceiling.

"What are you doing in my house?" he asked.

"I told you to stay away from my daughter, old man," Sam's mother said.

"Get out of my house."

The woman cackled a raspy sound, the remnants of a thousand and one smokes and tokes.

"Um, you're in no position to negotiate," she said. And then her eyes did something strange, something so unexpected that Elmore didn't realize his problem until it was too late. The eyes. They told everything. The truth. The lies. And everything in between.

The mother's eyes told the truth, as bitter and unfair as it was. They flicked, not to Elmore, but to a point over to his shoulder. He'd seen that look before, a VC happy that his comrade was lying in wait.

To Elmore's credit, he got halfway turned when the blow came, blunt but smashing. And as he crashed to earth, he heard Sam's scream. And once again, everything turned black.

CHAPTER FORTY-NINE

The pain hit first, the nausea next. He retched to the side, his insides emptying onto the hardwood floor.

He lay there panting, trying to regain his bearings.

He was home. He was lying on the floor.

He remembered slowly. Sam. The mother. The blow.

He retched again, more at the thought than the pain. Or was it the other way around?

No Sam now. No mother.

He eased his way into a sitting position. The front door was closed now. But the place was a mess. When he was finally able to get to his feet, head pounding, stomach churning, he saw the reality of what he'd been left with. They'd ransacked his house. A vase was gone. The set of Wusthof knives from the kitchen. The china set in the pantry.

Merely *things*. He didn't care about things. But he did care about memories.

The mother and her companions had smashed almost every frame in the house. The picture of young Elmore and his mother at Parris Island graduation. The picture of him and Eve two years before, waving goodbye to the cruise photographer before heading off to Alaska.

And there was his favorite, the one of the day he'd first met his beloved.

Elmore bent down, picked up the cracked frame. He dusted off the pieces of glass from Eve's smiling face.

How often do you really *look* at a picture?

He sat down on the couch with it. And back he went, through the years, to the day his life changed again.

———

HE'D NEVER BEEN to Central Park. Hell, he'd never been to New York City. He was curious of course. He wanted to walk every inch of the place. Just home from Vietnam, his legs were strong enough to carry him from coast to coast. Central Park was nothing.

His handlers had told him not to walk the city in his uniform. There were too many protesters, too many people opposing the war. There was bound to be a fight.

Cpl. Elmore Thaddeus Nix didn't care. He'd earned the right to wear the uniform.

Besides, if there was a fight on the horizon, so be it. He'd bested enough men in combat. What might a few New York hooligans really offer in the way of a brawl?

So he set off, attired in his greens, medal stuffed in a back pocket. No need to wear that. He'd place it in the first trash bin he found in Central Park.

As he made his way through the city from the nondescript first-class establishment some donor had paid for, he ignored the stares. He even ignored the praise, or the odd, "Semper Fi, Marine." Numb.

By the time he made it to Central Park, he thought the

fight he was looking for might never happen. The march had been more to prove himself superior to the draft dodgers and hooligans than a tour through the grand city.

He found them on the steps into the park, a ragtag band of longhairs decked out in cutoff olive drab fatigues. They spotted him moments later, eyes going cold.

"Baby killer!"

Cpl. Nix kept walking, ignoring the jabs. He'd heard about quieter places in the park. Places where a person could sit and nap if they felt safe enough. Places where artists often went to take up their craft. Places where darker deeds could be done.

There was a certain pattern to every place in the world. Elmore had found it in his humble hometown. He'd found the pattern in Vietnam, the way the rice paddies turned to valley and then the sudden rise of hills. That meant he found it in the heart of America, smack dab in the middle of Central Park.

There was the bridge archway, a dark place, out of the sun. A perfect place for a drug deal. The place smelled of a thousand such transactions.

He didn't hide. He stood right under the center point of that bridge, relishing the cool air. He stared into the future, into the past, into himself. He knew he'd never make it here. He'd lost himself somewhere over the mountains. He'd lost them not in country. No. That's where he'd found himself. He'd lost himself on the way home, when they'd ripped him away from his Marines, away from the only thing he'd ever truly understood.

Here he stood now, looking for the only confrontation in a three-block zone. He felt it keenly, the prickle of testosterone – a siren's call.

"You picked the wrong place to visit, soldier boy," came the first call.

Cpl. Nix recognized it as the voice of the tallest man he'd seen, the first to pipe up when the Marine had walked by earlier.

"Yeah, why don't you get your jive ass back to Vietnam?" said another.

There were laughs. Cpl. Nix didn't move. He was still facing the other way. If only they could've seen his face they might've moved on.

"You gonna drop some napalm on us, baby killer?" said the ringleader.

Cpl. Nix imagined his fist smashing the man's nose. He tasted the satisfaction.

The next words didn't come from behind. They came from above. A woman's voice.

"Leave him alone."

Everything shifted. Cpl. Nix moved, turned around to face the six men who'd come to join in the fracas. The six horsemen of the apocalypse.

Their gaze was half-fixed on him, half looking up, and then right, like they were tracking something or someone.

And then there she was. The sun cut through the gloom and escorted her down the dirt path that led to the concrete upon which the others stood.

Cpl. Nix stared. He couldn't help it. The way she strode so confidently, like the mere sight of six combatants didn't mean a thing. She looked so dainty and yet the strongest person he'd ever seen. That fire in her eyes. The eyes. They told you everything.

"You want me to get the cops?" she said to the others.

"What are you, a narc?" one of the combat hippies said, a

man with a mustache so bushy that it covered his mouth. "Buzz off, you fascist bitch."

"First of all," she said, "read your history books for the definition of a fascist. Second, I will not buzz off. Third, if you really had any principles, you'd go and fight for women's rights. I mean, if you really wanted to fight for anything. Otherwise, you're just a bunch of lazy squares with no purpose in life." Then she turned to Elmore, the first time she looked straight at him. "Are you okay?"

The words wouldn't come. Every ounce of pain he'd been feeling for weeks, from the announcement in that dirty hooch, the trip home, the Medal of Honor tour, it all melted away.

"Yes, Ma'am. I'm fine."

She put her hands on her hips and looked at the others.

"There, you see? We're fine. Why don't you all go protest something worthwhile?"

Not a question. A command.

"Last warning," the leader said. "Stay out of our park."

"Yeah? Go and get your title deed and we'll skedaddle," the girl said.

Elmore watched in dumbfounded amazement as the boys left the park.

"Have fun with your baby killer, 'Mrs. Nixon'," one of them tossed over his shoulder.

"Idiots," she said to Elmore. "I didn't even vote for Nixon. I'm so sorry about that. I hope that's not your only homecoming."

"No, Ma'am," was all he could get out of his mouth.

She turned, leveled him with those eyes.

Good Lord, those eyes.

"Well, if that's all."

Her eyes lingered over the ribbons on his chest, like she knew what they were.

"Thank you," he said, the words sounding impotent.

"It was my pleasure. My... my... where are my manners?" She offered her hand. It was the most beautiful hand Cpl. Nix had ever seen. He took it tentatively. Her hand was silk smooth and her grasp was firm. "I'm Eve. Eve St. John."

"Hello, Eve," he was just able to say, the word sticking in his throat like a spoonful of peanut butter.

She looked at him expectantly. Then she asked, "And your name is...?" She was smiling at him now, teasing with her eyes.

"Wha... Sorry, I'm Elmore. Elmore Nix."

He did his best to straighten.

Pull yourself together, Marine.

That's when he noticed that they were still holding hands. It felt like a lifeline to the world. It's how he would always feel from that day onward.

"It's a pleasure meet you, Corporal Elmore Nix."

That surprised him. "You know Marine ranks? I met some high muckety-muck last night at a gala that he paid for and he called me Sarge."

She shrugged. "My cousin was a Marine."

Was. There was nothing to say to that. Lost in the war like so many others.

She looked down, then up to his face. "Do you mind if I have my hand back?"

He felt his whole body flush and let it go immediately.

"You know," she said, "if you really want to hold onto me that badly, I could just walk next to you."

She stared into him, touched his soul with whatever power she now had over him.

"In fact, somewhere around here there's a vendor that

sells the best dogs in the city. How'd you like to help me find him?"

"Deal," he said, so consumed with her that he wished the world might end at that very moment. If it did, his life was complete, the masterpiece of God's plan.

So they walked, and she told him about life in New York City. Her family lived just off the park; somewhere she called the Upper East Side. She'd come from money. Her mom had met Jack Palance outside of Bloomingdale's. The library was nice and maybe they should go there next. The war was terrible and she hated it, but she was grateful for the men who fought.

Nothing would tear her from him.

Until life did.

HE PUT the cracked picture frame back in its spot. Eve had saved him that day.

It was time for him to pay it forward.

CHAPTER FIFTY

Sgt. Franks came with friends. Two retired lawyers and three ex-cops, one who'd gone on to the FBI until retirement.

There were suggestions to get the authorities involved. That was the obvious answer. Elmore didn't want to take that route. Sam's mother had the look of a career criminal, someone who knew how to skirt the law and use it to her own advantage.

It was Franks who took over the planning. "Look, Nix, I know this girl is special to you and all, but..."

"No. I'm not letting her go."

"That's not what I was about to say. My, you've developed a temper." But the jab came with a smile.

Something about the feeling in the room. Six Marines prepping for combat. The circumstances were merely a change of scenery. They were brothers in arms. Brothers forever.

"Sorry," Elmore said, though he was ready to press forward. He knew the motel where they lived.

"So, what's the plan, Nix? Run in guns a-blazin'?"

Elmore smiled. "What do you think I am, stupid?"

Grim nods all around. Time for something... *special*.

CHAPTER FIFTY-ONE

Sam sat in the corner of the empty room, hugging her knees to her chest. She was all cried out. The tears were only streaks of salt down her arms and legs.

Was Elmore okay? He'd been lying on the ground and it didn't look like he was breathing.

Jesus, if he's dead...

They'd taken her kicking and screaming. She'd bit through the finger of one of her mother's lackeys and gotten a punch in the stomach for her efforts. It left her gasping for breath as they stuffed her into the car and drove away.

Away from Elmore Thaddeus Nix, who very well might be dead!

She had no idea where they were. Not the same motel. *Another one?* Somewhere new. Somewhere dark and away from the sounds she was accustomed to. It felt more like an old office building, or maybe one of those warehouses that has its offices in the back.

She didn't know how long she'd been there. They'd taken her phone. The only thing ticking the time away was her breathing, and the occasional sniffle.

What would Elmore Thaddeus Nix do? She asked herself now, over and over. WWETND?

He'd become an integral part of her life. The only part that made sense. The fact that she'd made it through her parents' separation, through the abuse, and through her mother's illegal business was a testament to the human spirit that was always looking for something better. Elmore had been something better. An angel touched down in the most basic way.

Sam thought back to the day she'd met him. He, handing her a grocery bag. She, shying away like a wounded animal, ready to lash out should he even think of touching her.

He can't be dead. Please don't let him be dead.

She didn't know God in the traditional sense. But she knew God instinctively. She'd even sat outside the church around the corner from the motel and listened to the preacher hailing the glory, soaking in the praise of worship, the singing of the choir and the exultation of the congregation.

She knew God, but why wasn't God helping her now?

Rather than feel sorry for herself, she decided to plan. She would have the opportunity. They couldn't keep her locked up forever. She would get out — somehow. And when she did, she would find out what had happened to Elmore. If he was dead, she would leave town. Sam had learned that there were thousands of ways to leave. She could take a train, bus, Uber... She'd done the research. That was before Elmore. It was one of the reasons she'd been at that bus stop, to see how it all worked. The card in the store was going to be the goodbye to her mother. It was ironic that a woman who'd done so much to cause Sam pain was her mother, someone Sam still felt a deep love for.

The card. The bus stop. Elmore Thaddeus Nix.

She'd made the decision to stay, and then everything else had happened.

It's okay, she told herself. *You've gotten yourself out of messes before. You'll do it again.*

So she sat. She waited. And she prayed.

CHAPTER FIFTY-TWO

The motel was a bust. One of the old Marines, a former detective, rented a room for cash and did some digging. No one had seen Sam since the day before. That information had cost a hundred bucks and a pack of smokes.

"What now?" Elmore asked the former cop.

"Now we spread the net. I still think we need to alert someone. There are protocols..."

"No. We do this ourselves."

"Fine. Fine. Just making sure. Now, if it were me at the desk again, I'd scour the neighborhood. I think between us we can cover a block at a time in teams."

The plan was organized in the old way – simple and to the point.

They went at it in teams like they did in the old days, only now it wasn't hamlet by hamlet, but building by building. They had a picture of Sam from an online yearbook. A clever Marine who had spent his days with Missing Persons found it.

The search went on for most of the day and into the next. Elmore never slept, and the others only returned home to check on their loved ones, grab a shower and new clothes.

By sunrise of the second day, they were gathered in Elmore's kitchen again, ready to hit the pavement. Elmore was ready. He'd prayed, thought, and prayed again. This was the day, he could feel it.

"I made a call," Franks said, putting the last coffee mug into the dishwasher. Elmore froze. "Now, before you go off on me with that well-worn temper, Nix, I'll say that my friend took the call under the condition of anonymity."

Elmore couldn't breathe for a few beats.

"How do you know that?"

"I just do."

"That's not good enough. What if Sam's moth—"

Franks put up a hand. "She won't." He looked around the room. "The man I called, he's a friend. And to let you know that he is trustworthy – and I might mention that I could supply you with the proof – he's my sponsor."

"Your sponsor... as in...?"

"Sober twenty-three years now." It was said matter of-factly. No bragging. Just what it was. "So, my sponsor, he's... Well, let's just say he has certain skills that might be useful in our current predicament. He's willing to help if you agree to bring him in."

Everyone looked to Elmore. Cpl. Nix. United States Marine. Suddenly in the decision seat again. What choice did he have?

"Fine. Tell your friend we'd welcome the help."

CHAPTER FIFTY-THREE

Sam's stomach groaned. She was starving and thirsty. Even a sip of water would've been nice. A nibble of bread even better.

She adjusted her position, still posted in the corner where she could see every angle of her prison. There'd been noises, some music, laughing. Her mother's laughter.

Sam knew that laugh. Her mother was either high or drunk. Probably both. She never laughed when she was sober. The words coming out of the sober mouth always sounded wilted and tired. Sam thought about shuffling over to the door to listen, but that was too much of a risk. What if someone burst in?

So she sat and waited. Sat and thought.

She was midway into a perfect daydream, a trip to the beach, her first, when the door burst open and her mother stumbled in.

"There she is, my pretty little princess." The words felt like slaps. "You hungry, little princess? Want some food?"

Sam didn't want to answer. But the grumbling of her stomach in response to her mother's questions ruled over.

"Yes, please."

Her mother leaned back to the door.

"Hey, bring that shit in here."

A man, the one who'd hit Elmore over the head, came in the room. Sam tensed. At least she could deal with her mother. Her mother never touched her and made her squirm. She had her men do that for her. It was part of her deal with the devil.

"There's none left," the man said, wrapping an arm around her mother's waist, hand resting on her bared navel.

Sam's mother pushed him away halfheartedly, giving him a languid slap in the process.

"Then go get some more," she said. "I can't let my baby go hungry."

She was middle high. That's what Sam thought. Middle high was almost normal mom. Middle high mom didn't yell, scream. She tried to act like a proper parent. It was sober mom and too high mom that scared Sam. Maybe she could use this.

"I can go get it," Sam offered. "Just need my wallet."

Her mother took her tongue out of the man's mouth long enough to give her daughter a bored stare. "Nope. You stay right where you're at, little princess."

Then they left. Left her to sit. Left her stomach to grumble. Left her to wonder which mother would be the next to appear.

CHAPTER FIFTY-FOUR

Franks' friend was a gold mine. He must've had access to cameras or some of the suburban technology grid. He didn't explain how he knew what he knew. In fact, the man looked like anything but what he was.

His name was Jerry, and his squat jiggle only complemented his constant smile. Elmore couldn't help but like the man. He was the exact opposite of what he thought his old friend Franks would need to get sober.

"I tracked them here, here, and here," Jerry explained as he motioned to points on a map they'd picked up at the closest gas station. "I'll keep at it until I know more."

"Thanks for your help, Jerry," Franks said, offering his hand which turned into a hug. These men were not just friends. There was a deeper connection.

"It's my pleasure," Jerry said, releasing himself from the embrace. "And Mr. Nix, it was so nice to meet you. The old sarge told me all about you."

Elmore didn't know what to say, other than, "Thanks."

Jerry nodded at Elmore and then the others. "I'll be in touch."

When he was gone, Franks regained command of the room.

"Okay. Now we know we've been looking in the wrong part of town. I suggest we get back at it."

No one disagreed. Elmore was starting to think that maybe the others were right, that the authorities needed to be involved. But he couldn't make himself do it. He couldn't explain why, then or ever. Not to himself or out loud. He just felt it.

But he also felt like Sam's time was running out.

CHAPTER FIFTY-FIVE

Night came, and the food didn't. Sam's stomach had gone from groaning to moaning. She tried to ignore it by imagining all manner of vacations. To the mountains. To the beach. To the Taj Mahal.

The laughter and music still came from the other room. Loud sometimes and hushed at others.

At some point, despite her unease, and despite the hunger, Sam fell asleep. She drifted to a place far away. Far away from the past. Far away from her mother. Walking next to Elmore Thaddeus Nix. His wife was there. *Eve*. She smelled like Sam imagined she would, like springtime. And looked the way she looked in the pictures that her mom's goons had smashed.

Sam tried not to think about those, what Elmore must be thinking if he was still alive. She thought about the box she'd found in the closet of the guest room. High on a shelf, she'd had to fetch the rickety chair from the old desk in the corner. The box was heavy, weighed down by piles of papers – or so she thought. As she eased it down, she wasn't sure she'd be able to put it back.

The box wasn't some repository for household papers like bills or instruction manuals, it was full of memories. Decades of memories in their final resting place. Pictures. Letters. Postcards.

Through those memories, she'd learned of their love: Elmore and Eve. Two mismatched lovers who the universe had somehow, inexplicably stuck together. Eve wrote about it well, especially in those early letters. She marveled at what she called 'God's Plan' and how that fateful day in Central Park had changed them both forever.

Sam had never been to Central Park, but she imagined it now, food vendors, horse-drawn buggies, tourists clicking on their phones and cameras and the smell of roasting nuts. Such a strange and wonderful glimpse into Elmore and Eve's past.

She saw them now, walking hand in hand. Sam tried to catch up, but as in dreams, catching up didn't work. They never ran like Sam thought she was running; they stayed just out of reach. She couldn't hear what they were saying. Eve was doing most of the talking and Elmore was smiling. They didn't let go of each other's hands.

Something of Eve's letters had transferred to Sam's dream. She talked about how her favorite times were when she held her husband's hand, and they walked together in peaceful silence. That first time in Central Park. On the beach. In the car.

They were holding hands now in Sam's vision, inseparable. Then something happened – the dream shimmered, and husband and wife looked back at Sam with looks of utter confusion.

"Sam?" It was Elmore speaking, but his voice was different somehow. He was close and he reached a hand out and stroked her forehead. There was something alien about it all.

Something he would do. "Sam," he said, not a question this time. More urgent. Something about his voice.

Then his hand traveled from her forehead, down to her cheek, and then...

SAM AWOKE WITH A START.

"Hey, honey," the man said, his alcohol-laced breath sending waves of nausea through the girl.

She tried to scoot away. She tried. But his hands were on her now, pinning her in place, right in the corner.

"Let go," she said, though Sam thought her voice sounded gone, like it was calling from a cave muted with cotton lining.

"Baby, it's okay." He was touching her now. Touching her.

"No," she said, trying to squirm away.

He was too big, too strong.

Down the hands went.

Somehow Sam was able to twist just right, and her leg shot up, smashing into his privates.

He grunted and, reflexively, doubled over. His eyes swirled, and before she could squirm out of reach, his hands went to her neck.

Her vision wavered, but she kicked again. He moved. She kicked a third time. The pressing on her neck went from strong to a bit weaker. She couldn't breathe.

She kicked and she kicked.

"Hey," said her mother from the doorway. "What's...?"

Sam's foot hit home once again. The man stumbled back, hands flying from Sam's neck to his crotch. This time, he wailed like a wounded dog.

"You idiot!" Sam's mother said, but there was no anger like there should've been. No, she was laughing, first no more than a chuckle, then with a high pitched cackle. "She's made of tougher stuff than you!" The man slunk from the room, receiving a wobbly kick in the rear from the laughing mother.

When the tears were dried and the laughter gone, Sam's mother stood over her daughter. "Look what you did. You're more trouble than you're worth."

And then she turned, walked out the door, leaving Sam to the emptiness of her life.

CHAPTER FIFTY-SIX

"I think we're close," Franks said. He'd said that more and more in the preceding hours. Ever the optimist, Elmore's former platoon sergeant's attitude had never wavered. Thank God for Marines, Elmore thought.

He was a nervous wreck, though he hid it well. He thought of Sam, of her mother, of what the mother's friends might do. Time was slipping away.

The call came minutes later. Franks grunted a couple of times and finished with, "Thanks."

He put the phone on the dash and pulled off onto the shoulder of the highway.

"My guy says he's ninety percent sure he knows where Sam is."

"Where?"

Franks told him.

Elmore didn't feel relieved. He only felt the anticipation of a final battle.

"Let's go."

"Now hold on. That's not the best part of town, you know."

"Can't be worse than Hanoi," Elmore said. "And if it is, I don't give a shit."

"The point of all this is to get her out safe, right?"

"Of course."

"Well, you think charging in like you're taking an enemy machine gun hole is the best way?"

"I don't care. We need to help her."

"Sure. But I think we need to call the cops."

Elmore saw the severity that was stamped on his friend's face. There was no getting around it this time.

"Fine. But let's get there first."

THEY ARRIVED at the apartment row just before nightfall. The placed looked deserted, until Elmore looked closer. A man stood beneath the busted front porch light. As Elmore watched, the man flicked his cigarette off the porch and pulled out another.

He suddenly felt like there were eyes all around, peeking from every window. A civilian sniper nest watching. Waiting.

"It's either apartment 5A or 6A," Franks said.

There they were. Closed doors. A brand-new door on 5A. Graffiti slashing across the door of 6A.

"Okay. Let's call in the cavalry."

They'd consulted the others, the former cops. They'd say a suspected kidnapping victim was in either apartment. That would do it. The police would have to show. Maybe they'd punch it up by adding a domestic abuse charge. Anything to get them on the scene.

But Elmore had played along enough. He grasped the car door handle and leapt out before Franks could protest. His feet hit pavement and he moved with a surety and strength that belied his age. He was a young Pfc. again, as sure about life as he'd ever been. He decided to go for the graffiti door first. A 50-50 shot.

He saw the smoking guy shift, watching. Not a move to hide. Confident in his safety. No matter. Elmore was no threat to the man.

"Nix," Franks hissed from the car.

Elmore knew he was faster than his friend. Bum hips were an easy thing to take advantage of. He also knew that Franks wouldn't want to make a scene.

6A loomed closer now, twenty feet. Fifteen.

The first gunshot made him pause. The second turned his walk into a jog. The third, fourth, and fifth sent him sprinting toward battle, to the enemy inside 6A.

CHAPTER FIFTY-SEVEN

MINUTES EARLIER.

Sam had listened harder this time. She knew the cycle of her mother's demons. The next time the man came in, her mother wouldn't be sane enough, or even awake to intervene. Sam had to do something.

No windows to climb out of. No vents to climb up and into like in the movies. There was one way out.

They hadn't locked the door.

Impossible when the lock was busted. But it didn't matter. She was a scared little girl to them. Obedient in the past. Always listening to her mother.

But that last invasion of privacy had switched something in Sam's mind. It was wrong on too many levels to comprehend. Suddenly, the injustices of the past bubbled to the surface like a roiling geyser. She felt the surge keenly as she imagined Elmore and what he would do in her place. She smiled at the thought. Levity in the place of pity. That was her way. She imagined him in the jungles of faraway Vietnam saving countless lives.

They'd pulled her aside at the banquet, many whispered voices, and told her how special she must feel to have such a hero for a grandfather. They were in awe of him, the man who'd befriended her through the simple act of buying a card and a bottle of Gatorade. This man who lived a quiet, simple life. This man who'd lost his wife and now lived...

No. He hadn't really been living. He had cancer and she knew he'd meant for it to take him.

But she wouldn't let that happen. Not then. Not now.

No. She had to get out and make sure he was okay.

She made her way to the door, cringing at the squeak under her foot, an old creak under the moldy carpet. She made it to the door without incident, opened it slowly.

There was her mother, passed out on a couch in the corner. No snores. Just dead sleep. It was the other person in the room that worried her.

But he leaned against the couch, head hanging, and television still blaring. Some cop show Sam didn't know. How fitting. She could use a squadron of police cruisers right about now.

The exit was all the way across the room. An endless stretch that looked like the length of the Mohave Desert. Barren except for the detritus of junkies and addicts. Beer bottles. Used needles. Plastic bags licked of their dregs. These were the familiar furniture of her childhood.

Sam needed her backpack. There it was, in the corner closest to where she stood. A couple of steps and the first strap was in her hand. She glanced at the man who had tried to fondle her. Still asleep. She lifted the pack, revealing a pistol underneath.

She almost left it. Almost.

Once she had her backpack on, she bent down, stared at the weapon for a long time. It could be loaded. It might not be. She didn't know. She didn't know how to check. When she lifted it up she did so tentatively, like it might go off at any moment untriggered. But guns were only weapons in a person's hand. The man on the YouTube video had said that.

She turned the heavy thing over in her hand.

If nothing else, she could club the man over the head.

Yes, that's what she'd do. Only if she needed to. She didn't want to hurt anyone.

Sam was careful not to put her finger on the trigger, holding the pistol how she thought she was supposed to.

She felt better about her position now. Even if she made it halfway across the room and the man woke up, she could still make it. Sam knew that now.

And she did make it halfway, tiptoeing just in case she made any noise over the rattle of the commercial jingle blaring from the TV. She made it halfway and the man woke up.

"Whoa, whoa, where the hell do you think you're going?"

Sam froze. It was the fondling man. She remembered his name now. Ken.

"I'm hungry," she said, not turning to hide the weapon at her side.

"Get the hell back in your room, you little skank," he said, more annoyed than worried, or so it seemed.

"I'm just gonna get some food. My mom—"

"Your momma's dead." The way the man said it. No humor. No nothing. Just words tossed in the air like a blown match.

Sam now turned and saw that he wasn't as torqued as she thought. Worse still, his eyes leveled like laser beams. A second pistol rested on his lap, one hand gripping it at the ready.

"You're lying," Sam said. She swore she'd seen her mother's chest rising and falling. She wasn't dead, just passed out. She was always passed out.

Now Ken grabbed the pistol, and stood – shakily at first, steadier once he caught his balance.

"Sorry, baby," he said. The way he intoned that second word. Too much yearning there. Sam knew what came next, so she brought up the pistol.

Ken laughed mockingly. "Well, look at Annie Oakley over here. So, that's where that shit went." He reached out his free hand. "Come on, baby, hand it over."

"No," Sam said, the pistol shaking in her hand. It felt so heavy now, too much to hold.

"It ain't loaded, baby."

"Yes, it is."

Another mocking laugh. "You a gun expert now?"

Ken took a step closer. Sam's finger nudged the trigger, unsteady but still there.

"I know it's loaded, you piece of shit."

Ken let out a smoker's laugh, half cough. "I like you, baby. You're feisty. Keep it up, you're turning me on. I can't wait to get you alone."

"Stay back, goddammit!"

"Keep up the dirty talk, baby. You'll grow to like me. I was a cop you know. Yeah, four years on the force. Best time of my life. Free money and free drugs whenever I wanted. Too bad for the piss tests though. I used to steal clean piss from the lab, until they got me." His words trailed off into a laugh. "Caught me yellow-handed."

He stepped closer, too close. "Give me the gun, darlin'. No sense hurting yourself, what with your mom gone and all."

Sam had been sneaking glances at her mother. Was it true? There was an unnatural pallor to her mother's once-beautiful face. But that's how it always was, wasn't it?

"No."

Ken must have seen Sam's glances, because he half turned and grabbed one of Sam's mother's arm. It was limp.

"See? Dead as Elvis."

He went so far as to pull her mother off the couch where she slid to the ground, not a move of consciousness. Not a hint of life.

Sam's finger curled around the cold trigger. "No."

"Darlin', I'm gonna take you for one last ride before I—"

Without warning, she pulled, over and over again.

Eight shots in total, though the ear-splitting booms blended into one. She'd closed her eyes during it. There was no way she'd missed. She wasn't a monster, but she done a monster's deed.

When she opened her eyes, she expected blood and gore, just like in the movies.

But what she saw was worse – Ken was standing before her, laughing.

"Stupid little bitch," he said, barely getting the words out.

That's when Sam saw the holes in the wall behind him. High, at least three of the eight shots in the ceiling.

Ken straightened up like he'd been jolted with electricity.

"Okie dokie. After that racket, the cops'll be here soon. Better get to business."

His eyes turned to shiny stones, and he regarded her the way a leopard regards a fawn. In the past, she'd zone out. Now, she just cried. Her mother dead. Her life gone.

Sam fell to her knees. She was a little girl again. Frozen to the spot. Why did her body do this during these awful times? Why did it have to freeze like this?

Too soon he was standing over her. He reached down and stroked the top of her head. Once. Twice.

She went numb. If she died now, it would be okay.

There was a crashing sound behind. The hand on Sam's head lifted and everyone living turned to regard the disturbance.

That's when Sam saw Elmore's face, hard and determined, as he bowled right into the room, right into the line of fire.

CHAPTER FIFTY-EIGHT

Elmore was sure his shoulder went along with the door. Luckily, he'd gone with his weak side, the left. He'd crashed through one door before. That was a long time ago when his body was lithe.

No sooner had he made it into the room when his gaze fell to Sam, crouched behind a man with a gun. He had the look of a historic loser, all worn like the backroads of some forgotten town on the outskirts of Phoenix, cracked and broken.

The gun. Watch the gun.

Elmore stumbled a step, and then regained his footing.

A couple more steps, he willed himself forward.

Elmore took him out with the other shoulder, just right, like a linebacker plowing right through a receiver at mid-field. He felt the *wooomf* of lost air release from the man's chest, smelled the breath of a million cigarettes and stale liquor.

But there was nothing he could do about the gun. It was sandwiched between them now. His aim had been perfect if it had just been about making the game-saving tackle. But this was a battle for life itself. The man had no breath in him, but hc had a gun, a reliable pistol that pressed into Elmore's chest.

For a split second, the old Marine thought about twisting to the side, trying to wrench the weapon from the younger man's grasp. It was too late. He knew that. He knew it as clearly as he'd seen the battlefield years before. He knew it as clearly as he'd known the one and only woman he'd ever loved was Eve St. John stepping into the sunlight in Central Park.

So, he did the opposite. He hugged the man close, pressed the hard metal towards himself. Relief it was. Strange and beguiling relief. This was what he'd been put on the Earth for. To live. To save. To one day die.

Take me now, he said to his Lord, his heart open, wishing he could say goodbye to Sam. But he couldn't find the spoken words. His lips couldn't move, let alone get the saliva to flow.

The explosion didn't come as a surprise. Neither did the seer of pain. But he felt the man's grip loosen. Elmore took the opening and slipped his own hand between them.

The weapon was slick with his blood.

The pistol twisted just so. The man grunted. Sam said something Elmore couldn't understand. "Let him go," maybe? Or was it "Go get the hoe."?

The pistol finally worked to Elmore's pressing, although it expelled another two rounds before he could get it fully pressed in the other direction. He barely felt them. So easy now. So easy.

One. Two. Three times he squeezed the trigger, pressing his own finger over the man's. They were almost face to face now. The mask he watched, that of a broken man who'd ignored his own doom recognized it now.

Two more shots, two more jolts of bodies intertwined.

A trickle of blood seeped from the man's mouth, and then, slowly at first, the man went limp and slid away.

Elmore released his hold of the man but not of the gun. Who had it been that'd told him never to let his gun fall? A Marine. It had to be. One of his instructors.

He looked up. Sgt. Franks was standing over him.

"Hello, Sergeant," Elmore said.

"Oh, God, Nix."

Elmore looked down, saw the mess there. He'd seen this much blood before, but it was the blood of others. Boys he'd carried through barbed wire. Enemies he'd bludgeoned with e-tools and rifle stocks.

Now it was his. His blood. His life.

Elmore shivered. He wasn't in pain.

"Sergeant, have you met Sam?"

"Sure, sure, at the banquet."

Elmore nodded. Happy. He wanted to pat his old friend on the shoulder. There were so many things to tell him. He wanted Franks to know how his confidence had been his school, his graduate studies of what a real man was. Proud in the right way. Always looking out for his men.

But the words... Well, here he was. Such a mess. But there wasn't pain. That was good.

Someone was talking. Elmore realized he'd zoned out, thoughts drifting somewhere. To eternity? That would be nice. Eve would like eternity. Such a nice place. Was it a place or a thing?

"Elmore Thaddeus Nix."

His name snapped him back. Sam's face hovering over his.

"Ah, hello, Sam."

"Hello."

Tears. Too many tears.

"Don't cry," he said. He wanted to give her a handkerchief, the one in his pocket. But he couldn't remember where his pocket was. Strange.

"I can't," Sam said.

"Can't what?"

"Can't stop crying."

"Oh," he said, almost dreamily. To dream. That would be nice.

"The ambulance is coming. Just hold on."

His eyes drifted to his chest, to where she was holding something, a blanket maybe, over the growing center of deep red.

"Okay, Sam. Okay."

"Hold on."

But he didn't know if he could. This was it. It had to be. He'd done his duty one last time. And it felt good. Sam was safe. Such a wonderful soul she was. Sweet and smart. He wished she was his granddaughter. *Did they have such things in eternity? No, not eternity. Heaven. Wouldn't Eve have saved him a place there?*

"Thank you, Sam. You take care of her, Franks. You hear me?"

The old sergeant's face wavered somewhere on the periphery. "Don't go talking that way, Marine. That's an order. We'll take care of her together, you old coot, you hear me? Now hang in there, the ambulance..."

Elmore didn't hear another word. But he saw her face. Sam. Sad and searching. So beautiful. So full of... what? Ah yes, *life*. That was his doing now. It was the right thing.

And then someone called to him.

Sleep, the voice said.

Yes, Eve, my forever heart, I think I should sleep now.

CHAPTER FIFTY-NINE

Nurse Edie Tomlinson surveyed the crowd that poured in like a tidal surge. At first, the emergency room nurse thought that maybe the nearby festival had been attacked by some rogue gunman. That was the times they lived in now. The hospital had been briefed about mass shootings. But when she saw that most everyone looked healthy, she wondered if that maybe a celebrity had been admitted.

No, it turned out to be a man named Nix. They were asking for him.

When Edie looked him up, she saw that he'd been flown in. Critical condition. Emergency surgery. A goner for sure. She'd seen plenty of those cases.

So, the police came, and the visitors were told they would be contacted. Who the hell was this Nix anyway?

But they didn't leave. They found a spot across the parking lot, a grassy patch where they congregated. Soon there was one of those picnic tents and then another. Folding chairs appeared.

"It's a damn block party out there," one of the orderlies said.

"Yeah," Edie said absently.

"Who is this guy?"

"Damned if I know."

"You think he's some kind of criminal?"

Edie shot him a look. "Why would you say that?"

"I heard them talking. Something about getting shot and killing someone else. Has to be a criminal, right? Mafia guys have people who flock around them like groupies."

Nurse Edie put her hand on her hip. "You watch too much TV. Go sweep the damn rooms."

A criminal? Mafia?

Why the fuss?

CHAPTER SIXTY

Dreams. Such wonderful dreams. Dreams for days, for years.

Elmore wouldn't remember them, but he did remember the feeling of being pulled through the end of a vacuum cleaner. The world came back that fast, his hair tingling, his whole body aching, screaming.

He exhaled and coughed. Something in his throat. He was choking. It was one of his only fears. Choking or drowning.

But he was a good swimmer. An expert thanks to all those hours in the lap lanes, cruising by older-timers and their languid strokes. Elmore was always steady, sure strokes that cut through the pool or waves in the ocean. Eve called him a beautiful swimmer. He didn't know about that, thought she was being too kind, but he liked it when she said it.

More choking, then a glint of light. So bright. Too bright...

"It's okay, it's almost out."

Elmore gagged, the breathing tube finally coming out.

He coughed, a dry, pitiful sound, even to his own ears.

That's when he recognized the pain again, all over. He grimaced, which made the pain worse.

Then a warm glow seemed to spread throughout his body. The tension left him and back to the dreams he flew. But even though he wanted to see them, he didn't want to go.

————

HOURS LATER, he came to again. Groggily, steadily.

"Lookee lookee. Nix is awake."

He knew that voice. Franks. Sergeant Franks. His old friend.

Elmore blinked. Thankfully, the room was dim and manageable for his sensitive eyes.

"How ya feeling, Marine?"

Elmore could see him now, a blob of light, semi-featured.

"What happened?" Elmore just managed to squeak out.

"Oh, you know, young Private Nix just had to go and play hero again."

"I don't remember."

"Doc says that's to be expected. May come back, then again, it may not."

Elmore's gaze shifted to the other figure in the room. Silent. Then the eyes came into focus. Sam.

"Hey," he said, his voice clearing a bit.

"Hey," she said. This wasn't the young woman he knew. This was some timid thing that had snuck into his hospital room.

Then he remembered. Bursting into the apartment. The man with the gun. Someone lying on the couch. Or next to the couch.

"Your mother," Elmore said.

"She's dead."

Elmore gulped, or at least tried to.

"I'm sorry."

Sam nodded.

What else could he say? Nothing. So he reached out his hand instead. She stepped closer and took the hand in hers. So warm. So full of life. He squeezed her hand, pulled her a little bit closer.

She finally looked at him, really looked at him. That was when she broke and came forward. It hurt when she laid her head on his chest. He didn't care. This was where they were supposed to be. Something had brought them to this very moment. And in that room, in that very instant, Elmore Thaddeus Nix knew that he would live to a ripe old age, watching the young woman clinging to him grow into something beautiful, something wonderful to behold.

"It's okay," he said, stroking her hair though her sobs. "It's going to be okay."

And for the first time since Eve's death, he knew he was telling the truth.

CHAPTER SIXTY-ONE

They didn't let him leave for close to a week. There would be three more surgeries. Franks told him his guts had been ripped to shreds and that the doctors had been paid overtime to put the strands back together. Just like a Marine to put it that way.

During that time, he had visitors, too many to count. It was obvious that the hospital staff wasn't keen to that fact, but it was the head of the hospital, a woman who'd spent her time in the service as a nurse, who finally put her foot down. Elmore was given a private room and visitors were allowed to come and go during daylight hours.

And the funny thing was that Elmore didn't mind. He delighted in seeing friends and strangers alike. He loved hearing their stories, how'd they'd come home from Vietnam in shock, sometimes falling on hard times, but here they were. Still kicking. Still alive.

There were tears, of course. How could there not be? But they were happy tears. Through it all, Sgt. Franks played sentinel, and Sam played constant companion. Franks had contacted her school and had her work delivered by a group of rotating volunteers every afternoon. Elmore insisted she do her work before they settled in for that night's marathon of *Breaking Bad* or *Modern Family*. They were shows that Sam loved, and had somehow convinced Elmore to watch too.

He knew this wasn't the end of Sam convincing him to try something new. He felt new, so why not go with that feeling?

It was close to his time of release, his brain going somewhat stir crazy, when Sam's pencil stopped scribbling and she looked up.

"I think you should talk to your son."

"I know," he said.

"I know you know. Are you gonna do it?"

"Let's put it this way. Maybe brushes with death are different when you're sixty-seven as opposed to seventeen. I don't know. All I know is that I don't want to go to my grave knowing I've been an ass for as long as I've been."

"Elmore Thaddeus Nix, that's the first smart thing I've heard you say."

On the morning of his release, Sam made a call.

CHAPTER SIXTY-TWO

They met in a coffee shop two hours away. They'd left town against doctor's orders. It had actually been Sam's idea. While she'd been on top of all the hospital's orders, even making sure the nurses were doing their jobs, she'd given this journey a pass.

"As long as we get to treatment tomorrow, I think it's okay," she'd said. By treatment, she meant his cancer treatment. While they'd been digging around inside him, they did a little extra prep work in consultation with his oncologist. He was a go for the next round. Thankfully, his sixty-seven-year-old body was said to be healing at a rate of a healthy forty-year-old man.

They pulled into the tiny parking lot off the two-lane highway. The coffee shop was situated up a few steps, offering the patrons sitting outside a magnificent view of the surrounding countryside. Sam said the place was called 'a hidden gem' by some online review site she'd picked the spot from.

"It's perfect," she said as they ascended the stairs.

"You're enjoying this, aren't you?"

He had to hold onto her arm. He was still weak and taking each step up in elevation hurt more than he'd like to admit.

"Of course. It's beautiful here."

He didn't correct her. He knew that she knew what he meant. She was enjoying the process as much as the scenery. This was her element, and he let her play it. If it helped with her own recovery, so be it. Besides, unless it involved her buying some all-too-revealing mini to wear to school, he was beyond denying her anything.

They made it inside, though he felt like he'd just climbed a mountain.

"You okay, Thaddeus?"

Elmore nodded, wiping his brow with the handkerchief he always kept stashed in his back pocket. Though this one was new, a welcome home present from Sam. This one said, 'Stubborn Marine. Stand aside.'

"I'm fine," he said, but his insides were jiggling like last night's Jell-O.

"I think that's them over there," Sam said, pointing to the other side of the joint that was no bigger than some shacks Elmore had had the pleasure of visiting.

"Them?"

Sam nodded, smiling. She pointed again.

That's when he saw his face. His son.

And Elmore cascaded to memories of old, years never forgotten.

CHAPTER SIXTY-THREE

They'd prayed about adoption for a long time. As a married couple in their twenties, they'd been positively robust in their desire to have children. They'd tried and tried. Finally, it was Eve who suggested they see a doctor.

It turned out they were physically incapable of having children. The doctor said they could try other methods, expensive methods, and once again, it was Eve who said it was God's will at work. How had she had such faith? He'd only had faith in two things, and one, the Marine Corps, had let him down in the end. The second, his wife, was what he put all his chips on. She was right more times than not. So why not go along with her vision of God? It sounded good, even if he didn't totally believe. She would believe for both of them.

So, they'd prayed. He thought it strange. She'd never asked him to pray, but on this she did. They prayed in the morning and they prayed before going to bed. Sometimes they held hands, Eve's words strong and up cast.

"Please, Lord, if it is your will, bring us a baby. We

promise to take care of him or her, to love that child until our last breath."

There were variations, but the core was the same. She never outright asked. She always mentioned God's will. Elmore didn't completely understand that. If he wanted a loaf of bread at the baker he just asked for one. Why not just ask God for a baby?

But Eve said that wasn't how it worked. You couldn't just order up a child like you did a burger at the local drive through.

So, the prayers had kept on for a good three years. Eve's faith never wavered. Elmore kept at it for her. He loved her too much to say that maybe they should give up. He could've turned the conversation by saying that maybe it was God's will that they shouldn't have a child. But how can you will ingly shatter the faith of someone you love?

So he resolved to be the one who held doubts for both of them.

Then, they got a call out of the blue from an old school pal of Eve's. They'd done some traveling as families, foreign ports of call in expensive ships. Her friend, Melanie Delaphont, still lived in Manhattan and volunteered at one of the hospitals near her high-rise penthouse.

"Eve," said Melanie, "there's a young girl at the hospital. She's there with her family and she has a baby..."

In less than an hour they were packed and on their way to the airport. The ticket was expensive and Elmore considered complaining, but one look at his wife said it all. Eve would've sold the house and everything in it just for the chance to have a baby.

And so, they'd gone, far from home, back to the place they'd met. Elmore gazed out the airplane window over Eve's lap and saw Central Park as they circled down.

Melanie met them at the airport, had her driver take their bags to the waiting limo. The only limousine Elmore had ever been in was during his Medal of Honor tour, and the damn thing reminded him too much of hearses and their cargo. But there was no hesitating, no suggesting that maybe a cab would do.

The drive seemed to take forever. Elmore couldn't believe the traffic. It made him want to go home. He wanted to tell Eve that this was a fool's errand, sheer lunacy to think that a girl and her parents would give away a perfectly healthy baby. Crazy.

But it wasn't. The story came to light as they drove.

"The poor girl was in an accident. Hit head-on by a drunk driver," Melanie explained. "Her parents weren't keen on the birth in the first place and now... Well, you can imagine what they must be thinking. Anyway, I'm so glad I was there. I just happened to be meeting with the head of the hospital. I'm on the board, you know, and have been for years. Doctor Samuels, he's a good friend of Father's. Well, he got called down for this 'situation', that's what they called it. We still had things to discuss, so I walked with him. I'm so glad I did. When I heard the story, I knew I had to call you."

"But how?" said Eve.

"I've taken care of everything. You said you wanted the baby and the baby is yours. The papers are signed. You won't even have to see the family."

That's when everything began to sink in for Elmore, like a weight dropped into the pit of his stomach. How could they do it? His job barely paid for the roof over their heads. Sure, there was the money from the Marine Corps, but they put that away for their retirement. Then to add a baby to it all? How much did formula cost? Didn't they need a crib? Would Eve have to go back to work?

He wanted to speak up. He had to. He almost did, but he'd waited too long. Before the words of his valid concerns surfaced, they were at the hospital, limo idling.

"Are you ready to meet your son?" Melanie asked.

THEY MET their son through the glass of the nursery. One of a dozen babies inside, lying like little loaves of bread.

That was when the strangest thing happened. Elmore would later question whether, in fact, it had actually happened, but that baby locked eyes on him, on Elmore.

His son.

And that was it. He was done. Cooked. Creamed. Taken.

So, he made the promise again. This time he said it like a priest blessing hallowed ground, "Lord, grant me the strength to raise that boy with love and everything that goes with it."

He'd said it in his head. Hopefully God heard. And then, as if she'd heard the words, Eve squeezed his hand and said, "I love you, Elmore Thaddeus Nix."

THE FIRST TIME he held the newborn, he thought he was holding nothing but an empty blanket. The 'thing' was so small, so fragile. But the nurses said he was healthy, ready to go home when the paperwork got straightened out.

They told him that it was wonderful that two strangers had come to take the poor thing, the baby boy who'd lost his mother. Shouldn't they have to take a lie detector test, a drug test, or something else? No, they said. He was all theirs. There was even a small procession as they were escorted out. The head of the hospital even shook Elmore's hand. Imagine that. And that wasn't all. Elmore was sure he'd seen tears in the older man's eyes.

But then again, hadn't he been crying, too? He had. Just on the inside. Tears, sudden and powerful. Tears of joy for the boy, *his* son.

CHAPTER SIXTY-FOUR

He didn't realize he'd been squeezing Sam's arm too tight until she said, "Ouch."

"What? Oh, I'm sorry."

He swiped his hand away, swooning for a second. He really had to sit down. Maybe it was the surgeries. Maybe it was the cancer.

No, he knew what it was. Weakness.

"I'm okay," he said, waving Sam's offered hand away. "Come on."

He led the way out the side door. His chest constricted and his legs felt like they might fall to pieces. He felt two hundred years old and as spry as a spring chicken, all at once.

The door opened and the sunlight blinded him. He raised a hand, trying to pick out his son through the glare. That's when their eyes met. Like the first time, only now there was something different.

There were two children there with him. One a girl of maybe ten. The other, a boy in toddler clothes sat on the ground, tugging at errant strands of grass. They momentarily distracted Elmore. Confusion set in.

"Come on," Sam said, grasping his arm and pulling him forward. She led the way, thankfully.

"You must be Sam," said Oliver Nix, rising to meet them. The man put up a hand. "Hi, Dad."

Dad. So much contained in three little letters. Purpose. Right. Responsibility.

Elmore nodded. "I'm afraid I'm a little less than what you expected to see."

The man smiled politely. "Sam told me what happened. You look fine."

There was a long stretch of nothing, just the sound of the little boy playing on the ground, humming some tune to himself. Sam was no help on this one. Whether that was by choice or indecision, Elmore didn't know.

"So..." Elmore started, meaning to ask about the children. Meaning to start anew.

"I only came for Mom," Oliver said.

There it was. The truth. He didn't want to see his father. And beneath the hurt, Elmore understood that. He understood it like he expected the sun to rise each and every morning. There were things you could forget, things you could forgive. Then there were others...

"I understand."

"Was she in pain? You know, when she..."

"No, son. She wasn't in pain."

Son. He wanted to say that over and over again, until the air left his lungs and his mouth dried like the desert.

Oliver nodded. Elmore noted that his son looked good, handsome and healthy. Eve would've said he looked very put together. He wore a simple T-shirt and jeans, but Elmore could tell they were worth something to anyone who cared. His son had money.

"There are some things I'd like to have of hers."

Oliver, thirty years old now, sounded like a teen again. Always close to his mother.

But he and Elmore had been close too. That was before the thing. Before the bitter words that tore their relationship apart like crepe paper.

"Of course. Whatever you'd like."

Another long stretch of silence. Then someone else walked up. An unfamiliar face, handsome and perfectly setup like he'd stepped out of a men's magazine for high-end wear. He grabbed Oliver's hand and slipped it in his own.

"You must be Mr. Nix," the stranger said.

"Hello," Elmore responded.

There were so many things he wanted to say. So many. But the words wouldn't come. Damn, why wouldn't they come?!

"Well, I think it's best if we get our son home for his nap," the other man said.

There were nods all around. Even Elmore nodded dumbly, like a deaf mute who'd just been sent to the gallows and didn't know why.

And before he knew what was happening, they were gone.

Elmore sat down at the table once occupied by Oliver and the little girl. His heart felt like it would cave in on itself.

God, why?

Sam sat down across from him, took his hand.

"You knew it wasn't going to be easy," she said.

"Sure."

She squeezed his hand.

"Elmore Thaddeus Nix, tell me you're not giving up."

He looked up from his pity at those blazing eyes.

"What?"

"I said you're not giving up. *We're* not giving up."

"But you didn't say anything. Why didn't you...?"

He stopped speaking at the look she was giving him. Like

a school mistress who'd just caught her pupil in a bold-faced lie.

"This is your fight, not mine."

He wanted to grumble, to tell her that she'd dragged him all this way. And for what? To be reminded of all the pain? To be shown that he really was a failure?

Then he saw the truth. You can lead a horse to water...

"I messed up."

Sam nodded. "Yeah, you did. So what?"

"So you think there's a chance?"

"Of course, there's a chance. There's always a chance."

He couldn't help but smile. "How did you get to be so wise?"

She just shrugged. "Must be a brain defect."

CHAPTER SIXTY-FIVE

The next day it was back to treatment. They really did try to make the place comfy. There were magazines, tablets with movies and TV shows if you wanted. There was even the smell of something homey, something from his past that Elmore couldn't pinpoint. Pie maybe?

But no matter how they tried to mask it, the place reminded him of death. Death warmed over with treats and soda, but still death.

"How much longer?" he asked Sam who'd taken a tablet and was watching some show on YouTube.

"Fifteen minutes," she said without looking up at the clock.

He exhaled and tried to relax. This wasn't the hard part. The stink of it came later. The nausea. The tiredness. He'd had a taste of it before, before the mess with Sam's mother. But now, well, he really did want to get better. His son would be coming in a few days and he wanted...

What did he want?

For those last fifteen minutes, he tried to think on it. He

tried to figure out the future. But as usual the answers didn't come. Either God wanted it to be a surprise or a test.

He remembered a line from a Woody Allen movie: "If He's gonna test us, why doesn't He give us a written?"

The machine next to him buzzed and moments later a nurse appeared.

"You're all set, Mr. Nix."

She was all business and smiles as she detached him from the death device. *The damn thing was made to kill. Kill cancer for sure, but it could just as well kill me. Imagine it. A torture device in plain sight.*

"Take your time, if you'd like," the nurse said. He thought her name was Rachel, or was it Rita? Maybe his memory was going too. And for a harrowing minute, he wondered if that was one of the side effects, losing your memory. He went back through the checklist. Nausea. Restlessness. Exhaustion. Lack of appetite, on and on. Had the doctors and nurses mentioned memory loss? How would he remember if they had?

He couldn't lose the memories. They were all he had. They were his fuel.

"Are you okay, Mr. Nix?" the nurse asked.

"Um, yes."

"You went pale for a minute."

"Oh, I'm fine."

She had the look of someone who was about to correct him, maybe say that everyone tried to act tough. But she didn't.

"You take it easy for the next couple of days."

"I will," Elmore said, wanting to be gone from this place. Why did the death smell feel stronger today? Was the reaper around the corner? Had they changed the potpourri?

He felt fine walking down the hall. He felt fine climbing

into the elevator. He felt fine climbing behind the wheel and heading for home. Their home. His and Sam's now. That was official. It hadn't taken much.

Just the death of a mother, Elmore thought.

He didn't feel fine when they pulled into the neighborhood. He felt even worse as he gripped the front door handle. Now his body reeled and it was everything he could do to open the damn door and step into the delicious coolness of the conditioned air.

Sam lagged behind or she would've seen his face. That would've given him away, his pallor, his pain.

He gulped down the bile. "I think I'm going to take a nap." He was quick for the door.

"I got the mail," Sam said behind him. "You got a letter, I think it's from..."

But Elmore didn't hear the rest of the words as he slammed the bathroom door and knelt for the forthcoming tsunami.

CHAPTER SIXTY-SIX

'Oliver Nix', written in that familiar handwriting, along with an address that must've been some well-to-do neighborhood. He touched the X in the Nix, noting the familiar way his son still curled the end of it.

He flipped the envelope over and over in his hand. Sam hadn't opened it. He wished that she had. If it was bad news, she'd know how to soften the blow. Yes, that was it. He'd give it to Sam and let her read it.

Before laying it down, the envelope flipped two more times in his hands, mimicking the motion of his stomach hours before. After his fit in the bathroom, sleep had come quickly. His body wouldn't allow even a word. Sam understood that, and the envelope with his son's handwriting sat waiting when he awoke sometime late in the night.

It was just after midnight. A new day. Was that some sort of omen? Had God wanted to clean out his guts before he felt the cruel sting of his son's words?

Suck it up, you old coward, he told himself. And he really was being a coward. It was just a letter. Just a bunch of words. How much could it hurt?

But he knew. Elmore Thaddeus Nix knew that words, or even the lack of words, could be just as deadly as an axe to the head. Words had the innate ability to nuke, maim, slice, and dice their way into your soul.

Open it.

Live.

He slipped a fingernail under one corner, slowly, carefully. His entire life now focused on this singular effort, so simple. The way the flap popped up surprised him. He half-expected a specter to float out and devour him.

Great. Now I'm having living nightmares.

No specters came forth, but he thought he detected the subtle hint of... no, it couldn't be. But the nose told of the memory.

My God, that's Eve's perfume.

He put the envelope to his nose and closed his eyes and breathed it in until his lungs were full of it.

Now his hands fumbled with the parcel, eager to find what was inside.

There were two notes. One on thick paper, something you might buy at some high-end stationery store, something on 5th Avenue in New York City. The second was smaller and a bare blush of pink. He recognized it instantly. It was Eve's.

He opened Eve's first, gulping when he saw her handwriting.

Elmore, my darling,

I can't imagine what you must be thinking. I'm sure you miss me. I know you do. All I can say is that I love you, that you were one of the most important pieces of my puzzled life. Remember the puzzles we used to do, thousands of pieces? Well that's life. I know you might not like that. You like things simple, black and white. That's why I love you. I love you so much. I've loved you from that very first moment. You in your perfectly tailored uniform and me and my terrible temper and those boys in the park.

My Elmore, I'm sure our love is one for the ages. One that God treasures. But there is another that we lost. One that we both screwed up. Our son, Oliver. He is our son. We were wrong to let him go. We were so wrong.

Love him, my dear. Love him until your last day. For I love you, I love you both so much.

Live, Elmore. And love.
Yours for eternity,
Eve

He couldn't stop the tears if he tried. They came after 'darling' and kept coming well through his third reading of the note.

Oh, my Eve. My Eve, he said to the heavens.

How had Oliver gotten the letter? Had his wife mailed it to their son? Only one way to find out.

He opened the second letter.

Dad,

Mom sent me this letter. I can only guess that it was soon before she died. I was there you know, at the funeral. I wanted to see you, but I hid. I'm not proud of that fact. But I was there to see mom. I wanted you to know that.

I thought I knew what I was going to say, but every time I read Mom's note... well, I'm sure you can imagine.

Did you know that she used to call me once a day? Every day since the day I left. The day you let me go.

I never picked up the phone. She always left a message. She always said the same thing: "I'm sorry and I love you."

Can you imagine? Over ten years and she never missed a day until she died. That's when I knew. When the call didn't come, I just knew.

That's my fault. That's something I have to live with now. She tried to make amends. She tried.

So there's that. Do with it what you want. As for me, I don't know what I want. I guess I just want to move on and remember her the way she was.

I love her. She loved you. That's it.

Oliver

The walls felt like they might crumble and bury him alive. First Eve's note and then this. Elmore had no idea what it meant. Maybe Oliver didn't know. All Elmore did know was that it confirmed every idea he had of what his son thought of him.

And to be fair, he agreed with every silent accusation.

CHAPTER SIXTY-SEVEN

I t had been a day like any other. Elmore came home from work, tired but satisfied. He liked the feeling of a job well done, always had. It wasn't until he'd stuck his shoes in the bin in the laundry room that he guessed something was amiss.

"Eve?"

"We're in the kitchen."

He clomped his way in, his feet stiff from being upright most of the day. Oliver and Eve were sitting at their small table. The boy was home for the summer. He'd just graduated from college, something both parents were proud of. The Ivy League had made quite the dent on their savings, but the medal and some scholarships along the way had helped. Elmore had felt like a fish out of water going to that graduation, what with all the pomp and prescription, but it was all for Oliver. His plan was to go to New York City. Eve's friend Melanie, who was Oliver's godmother, had offered to give the young man an extra room in her house. Extra room! The place was a mansion. It was more like an extra wing.

Elmore stepped up to the kitchen table. "Hello." He didn't pry. If there was something they wanted to tell him, they would in due time. Oliver had a way of mulling, thinking things over, not unlike his father. But when words came, they usually came in a torrent, like a faucet he couldn't turn off. Elmore braced for it.

"Oliver has something to tell us," Eve said, resting a hand on her son's.

The boy sat upright, his face strong and resolute. "I'm not who you think I am." The words came out in a rush and it took Elmore a few seconds to piece them together.

"What do you mean?" Eve asked, well before her husband could form the words to reply.

There was a nervous smile playing around his face. "I'm not... I don't know how to say this."

"Just say it. It's okay."

"I don't want to disappoint you," Oliver said.

"Why don't you just tell us and I'm sure we can work it out," Elmore finally said. He saw Eve nod, rest a second hand on her son's shoulder. Had he stiffened at the touch or softened? Elmore couldn't tell. He'd never seen his son so... *whole*.

"I'm gay."

The expected torrent never came. And the rush of silence couldn't have been there a second before. Elmore was sure of that. He didn't know what to say because he just didn't. When he looked back on that moment years later, he tried to figure out what he should've done.

He should've walked around the table and hugged his son.

He should've said everything was going to be okay.

He should've said he loved his son no matter what, and that as long as he was true to his friends, was honest and upright, loved his country, stood up for what he believed was right, put his ass on the line in service of the truth, and spoke that truth wherever he found himself, then he would be proud of him.

But he did none of those things. He acted the part of the court jester, dumb and slack jawed. The village idiot. The father who'd forgotten every glorious gift his son had given him. He played the fool and life caught him by the short hairs before he could get his jaw moving.

For some reason, Eve didn't say anything either. It was only later that Elmore realized that she was looking to him, her husband, to make the first move.

But he didn't.

"Are you sure?" said Elmore. It was innocent enough, he knew. But it wasn't what he should have said. He knew what he should have said.

Oliver's eyes blazed now, the same fire they'd seen so many times. Eve called it the Nix fire, and Elmore knew she meant the fire came from Elmore. That fire had seen him through his broken childhood, through Vietnam. Now the fire blazed against him

Elmore actually recoiled, and in that split second when he stepped back, he knew the action would be taken as an accusation. But he couldn't help it. He couldn't. No explanation ran from his soul, through his lungs, up through his larynx and out of his mouth. None. Zip. Zilch. Just dead air. Dead air between them.

"I knew you wouldn't understand." Oliver shoved himself back from the table, wresting himself from Eve's grip. Eve's mouth dropped open. "You're no better than the others!"

That fire. Elmore could barely look at it.

And that was it. Both parents were silent and Oliver was gone. Gone in a huff. Gone in a moment.

They only talked about it one time. That night Eve cried and Elmore said their son would come back. He was their son, after all. They always came back.

But he never came back. He never called.

Elmore didn't give a damn about his son's sexual orientation. Sure, he'd thought on it. He'd seen families ripped apart by it, but he'd never... Well, he'd just never thought it through. All he wanted was a boy who would grow into someone special, someone of worth to mankind.

The first time Oliver had left home, Elmore didn't sleep for three straight nights. It was a big bad world out there. Elmore knew. He'd seen it firsthand. Kids blown to smithereens because some despot gets a wild hair up his ass and another leader thinks he can smash said despot back to the stone-age. You don't want your child to be part of that. You have to protect them. You have to get them ready. You have to...

Have to.

Elmore knew he had to do something. But he didn't. That had been his fatal flaw, the regret he'd lived with for over a decade. And now here it was again, the devil digging his claws deep inside.

CHAPTER SIXTY-EIGHT

Elmore put the two letters down. Sam was standing next to him again. She didn't say anything, but Elmore figured she'd read the notes by now.

"I think I need to lie down," Elmore said, his body slack.

She motioned to the letters. "What do you want me to do with these?"

Elmore didn't answer. He somehow made it to his room, locked the door – the only time he'd ever locked it – and lay down to let sleep take him.

But sleep didn't come. Dreams did. Waking dreams that thrashed around in his head until finally, hours later, he drifted into the abyss of darkness.

PFC. Nix clawed his way up one last hillock. The top of the thing was covered in mud, like it would melt away as soon as he crested. So quiet. So damned quiet.

He looked all around. Sgt. Franks had just been behind him. They were going to take out a pair of sappers they'd just seen. Nix looked back down the hill, but the trail he expected to see was no longer there. Only nothingness, a color that wasn't a color. A space that wasn't a space.

Then the sound came. He thought it was machine gunfire from far off. *Tap, tap, tap, tap.* He cocked his head to one side. Probably VC probing friendly lines.

Tap, tap, tap, tap.

No. That wasn't right. It sounded like an American-made weapon. He'd committed most of them to memory. It was a game now. Hear a mortar round whistling in? Quick. Guess what size it is before it hits. Winner gets a Hershey bar or a beer on R&R.

Not that they ever really knew who the winner was. Not that it mattered. It was just one of a thousand ways to pass the time.

Tap, tap, tap, tap.

Closer now.

Tap, tap, tap, tap.

Nix looked around again. The nothingness surrounded him now. He didn't seem to mind that the trees were gone and the mud that once caked his hands had disappeared.

Tap, tap, tap, tap.

A knocking. Nix thought. And then he opened his eyes.

IT WAS DARK. Pitch black.

Tap, tap, tap, tap.

Moments that must have been seconds for him to get oriented.

He was home, lying in a bed.

Tap, tap, tap, tap.

A giddy fear gripped his chest. "Who's there?"

"It's Sam. Are you okay?"

Sam.

Elmore eased himself to the edge of the bed. "What time is it?"

"Almost three."

"In the morning?"

Of course, you old fool. It's dark out.

"Yeah, three in the morning. Are you okay?"

Elmore wiped a hand over his face. He felt like he'd been sleeping with his head in a cooler.

He got to his feet, pins and needles spiking the length of his legs. "You can come in."

"The door's locked."

Locked. Had he locked the door? He never locked the door. Not even when there was that string of break-ins some years back. When was that? Must have been when Oliver was still at home. Oliver. He wanted to see Oliver.

"Are you sure you're okay?" Sam asked.

Elmore was embarrassed to realize that he'd slipped again, the mental agility losing its battle to Father Time.

He unlocked the door, saw Sam standing there in an over-sized T-shirt and gym pants.

"Sorry. Didn't know I'd locked it."

The light of a car driving by splashed across the front of the house, dousing them both in a brilliant glare. Had he forgotten to close the front curtains? How careless.

He saw Sam's face, ghostly pale. He thought it was the light that was now passed, but her mouth was hanging open just so.

"Sam, what is it?"

"It's..." Her hand raised. She was pointing. Pointing at him. "We need to get you to the hospital." She'd recaptured a modicum of sanity and was moving now.

What the devil was she yammering about? Damn girl didn't know what she was talking about. Sure, he felt a little tired. Probably had some hair out of place, but that was no reason to get cagey. Maybe she was having a traumatic episode, something about her mother.

Then Elmore felt it, the uncharacteristic anger. Where had it come from? Tapped from some place deep down. Like someone had slipped it in when he wasn't looking.

He decided to splash some water on his face. That would do the trick. Then he would talk to Sam, see what was wrong. Maybe she needed a counselor. How could he have been so stupid not to see that coming?

"Idiot," he told himself, slapping the side of his thigh with a sting. "Water."

He shook his head on the way to the master bathroom. Maybe he was dreaming. If he was, he wanted to wake up. The next thing would be unicorns and dancing pixies. What the hell was a pixie anyway? He was seized by the urge to scream out an obscenity. He wanted to tell off his dreams, curse the world. Spit in Sam's face.

That's when he stopped. This wasn't him.

He hurried now. A flick of the light switch and there he was, standing in front of the double mirror, staring at a complete stranger. The man he was looking at looked a hundred years old, with a pinched face as bitter as a crab apple.

There were no other thoughts as he slipped to the floor, casually gripping the edge of the sink. A girl was screaming. And then the world disappeared, thankfully, dully, and completely.

CHAPTER SIXTY-NINE

S am didn't know how to pray. She'd never been taught.
But she prayed now, with every high and mighty
word she could think of. She gripped her hands together until
they lost blood flow. And still she prayed on.

*Please, God, save Elmore Thaddeus Nix. He's my friend. My only
friend. Please, God, I don't know what I'll do without him. I don't
have anyone. Oh, God, I don't have anyone.*

She didn't know the perfect prayer and yet she said it.
The words sprayed forth. Over and over the words went,
spilling from her until they could spill no more.

Doctors and nurses came and went. An orderly asked her
if she wanted anything to drink. She shook her head and went
back to praying.

And the hours went by.

———

"He could be out for a while," the doctor said to George
Franks.

"Tell me the truth, Doc." Franks leaned in close. He didn't want Sam to hear. She'd been through enough.

"That's all I can say. It could be a while – if he comes out of it."

Franks looked over at the girl in the corner. She'd been hysterical and composed all in the same minute. Raving mad and pointedly focused. She was a strange creature, this Sam.

"You have to understand," said the doctor. "It's in his brain now. We removed most of it, but we think there might've been damage."

Franks stared at the man. He'd lost friends before. He'd lost too many Marines to count. He liked to think that their faces were etched on his soul. He'd sent them to their deaths, even if he'd been under orders. He would've gladly given his life for theirs. Had tried on more than one occasion. But the good Lord had seen fit to keep him. He'd kept him through Vietnam, through a patchy homecoming, through alcohol.

His heart broke seeing Elmore Nix in that bed, head half-wrapped in bandages. Nix was the indestructible one. He'd run into gunfire and come out unharmed. He was a miracle. Franks honestly believed that.

So was this it? Was this when Almighty God took back his miracle?

No, it couldn't be.

"Okay, Doc, tell me what we can do."

And then, to Franks' surprise, the doctor said, "Pray."

So they prayed. He and Sam prayed together. They held hands and prayed to themselves and sometimes they prayed aloud. Visitors came in ones and twos, just like they'd come before. They prayed. They sang. They waited.

All the while, Elmore Thaddeus Nix lay in a coma, still living, even if on borrowed time.

CHAPTER SEVENTY

No dreams. No dreams at all. Just a canvas of white with the occasional splash of Easter color. A muted blue here or a barely yellow there.

He came in and out of it. Sometimes it felt like he was on a boat, far out to sea. There was no water, but the waves lapped him from side to side. Where was he going? Was that a seagull squawking? What were those other sounds? The sound of an engine maybe. Possibly the rigging of an old schooner squeaking in the wind.

Ah, maybe he was on a pirate ship. He'd like that. He'd had fantasies about being a pirate as a child. Curved scimitar leading the way as they attacked merchant vessels in the Caribbean. Yes, that was the life. Sunburned and guzzling grog from a silver tankard. Yo-ho-ho and a bottle of rum.

"Here he comes," the nurse said.

They'd taken out the breathing tube. There'd been signs

of life. Fluttering eyelids. The twitching of fingers and toes. More prayer. More movement from the unconscious patient.

Sam stood next to him, waiting, her eyes sunken from lack of sleep. She had not left the hospital in the past week. Where would she go even if she could leave?

Elmore's eyes moved around in their sockets, searching, feeling it out.

Sam bent over, put her mouth right next to his ear.

"Elmore Thaddeus Nix, come back to me."

More twitching. Something fighting to come out. There was a moan from somewhere deep down.

Sam moved back, fearing that she'd triggered the final death spasms.

"I'm sorry," she said, to Elmore, to Sgt. Franks who was always there, to the world.

Franks caught her, held her close.

"It's okay. Look."

He pointed at their friend. Elmore's eyes were fluttering now, baby butterflies.

And then his eyes came open, and he was with them again.

"Can I have some water?" Elmore asked, and Franks fell into a fit of laughter.

"You really had us worried, you stubborn old mule," Franks said.

Elmore was propped up, sipping from one of those over-sized water bottles painted some shade of mauve, that's what he thought it was. An antique castoff.

"I can't believe I'm so thirsty. I could really use a Gatorade, the kind with all the sugar. Not that G2 stuff."

"The doctor said you should stick to water, for now," Sam said. She hadn't left his side and Elmore wasn't sure he liked that look on her face. Worried for sure. But something else, like as if she felt he might die.

"Okay. Then water it is."

"You tell us when you're ready for visitors," Franks said, flipped through the newspaper, apparently no worse for his old friend's wakeup.

"Same as before?" Elmore meant his most recent stay in the hospital after getting shot. He was getting to be a real pro at this hospital bed thing. Maybe he'd rack up the frequent flier miles.

"Same and more," Franks replied, not looking up from whatever article had him so entranced.

Elmore shook his head, still finding it impossible to comprehend that so many could care so much about an old man.

"And how are you, Sam?"

"I'm good," she answered too quickly, like she'd rehearsed it.

"Really?"

"Yep."

"Had any good food?"

"Sure."

"Steak and eggs?"

That got her face to change. "No. Just hospital food."

"That doesn't sound very good."

"They make good pancakes. Really big ones. And sandwiches. The sandwiches are pretty good."

Franks threw him a look that said it all. Sam hadn't been eating. Maybe a nibble here and there. And all for what? An old man dying in a bed.

"That settles it. As soon as I get out of here, I'm buying

us the most expensive meal we can find," Elmore said, feeling suddenly energized. And besides the aches and pains of his aging body, he really did feel good. They'd told him about the brain tumor, how they'd scraped him out good. The doctor was cautiously optimistic. They were always like that. But Elmore saw the truth. He always saw the truth whenever his own demons weren't casting shade on it. There was a very real chance that he might die. First the cancer in his back and now in his brain. The fainting spells had shown the truth. Good. One step in the right direction.

"What d'ya say, Sam, a fancy dinner? You, me and that old goat in the corner?"

Franks looked up from his paper. "Who you calling an old goat? Look in the mirror, Gyrene."

"Sam?"

Sam's eyes glistened. No words came.

Elmore took her hand, made her look right into his eyes.

"Sam, I'm not going anywhere. I'm making this promise right here and now. As long as you're here with me, I'm going to fight this damn thing as hard as I can. I can't promise that I won't die. I won't insult your intelligence by telling you that. You're as much an adult as I am now. But I've decided to live. Eve taught me that and so have you." He stared at her, those beautiful eyes full of affection. "What do you think? Will you help me?"

And then, with a nod that turned into an ear-to-ear smile, Sam said, "It would be my pleasure, Elmore Thaddeus Nix."

Just like that, they decided to live, together.

CHAPTER SEVENTY-ONE

Once again, Elmore shocked the hospital staff. He went home in half the time. It might've been a stretch, but he knew that home was where he needed to be. Besides, he owed Sam and Sgt. Franks a fancy dinner, and that was impossible sitting in a hospital bed in a gown that didn't even cover his rear end.

Home they went. Sam moved into her old room and Elmore settled into the bed he'd shared with Eve since moving into the house. It felt different now, emptier, like the last vestiges of his wife's spirit had finally flown away. To heaven no doubt. There was no other place for a woman like Eve.

He smiled as he smoothed out the bedspread she'd brought home from Italy. She'd spent hours picking out just the right one. She liked bright colors that had no descriptive equal. Some might call it gaudy, but Eve loved it, and now so did Elmore.

That's when he realized it. He took a turn, then another, gazed all about the modest room. The tray that held her wedding ring on the bedside table had been a purchase in

Taiwan. It was a delicate thing, accented with jade. There was the picture frame they'd bought in Paris. It was a little too fancy for Elmore's taste, but now that he thought about it, it perfectly encapsulated their visit.

Everything. Every little detail. They were all memories. Reminders of their little adventures together.

Elmore looked up at the ceiling and sky beyond.

"Thank you, sweetie."

And the tears came, along with the thought that it was time to add to these memories. His wife was gone, but life wasn't.

THEY HAD dinner at a steak house that catered to the rich and famous. It took a few phone calls, but one of their number, a Marine who'd spent time in the state legislature, got on the phone with the governor, another grunt, who arranged his private table for the dining trio.

And grand it was. No less than four waiters treated them like kings. Homemade rolls that were as delicate as May flowers segued into an array of appetizers that made home cooking look like slop. And the main course, a delicately smoked, buttery filet the size of a football, and two delectable sides, expertly-crafted, was enough to send them to heaven.

By the time dessert came, Sam declared that she might never have to eat again.

They ate dessert nonetheless.

The entire meal went by without talking about death and dying. Instead, they talked of the future, of what they might do together, Elmore and Sam. Sgt. Franks had a life to get back to, but he said he'd consider their offer of coming along for the ride.

"I'm no spring chicken, you know."

"Have you seen me?" Elmore said. The two old Marines had a good laugh at that. It felt good to laugh, like he hadn't done it in a century or more. He promised himself that he'd do it more often. He'd take it all in, the good and the bad, and make it better. Life was what it was. It was all how you processed it. He had Sam to thank for that. She never ceased to amaze him, with her honesty, with her firm belief that life would go on.

Elmore raised his glass. "To great friends. May we cherish each other and never forget that it was here that time stood still."

"To life," they all said in unison, Sam giggling.

It felt good to be alive. It felt good to be home.

CHAPTER SEVENTY-TWO

The next two weeks ebbed and flowed with the tide of their new life together. Elmore drove to and from treatment, Sam always in tow. She knew each and every nurse's name by then. They loved her. They asked how she was doing and whether her grandfather was behaving.

Elmore loved the treatment for one very strange reason. Here, in a room filled with patients young and old, he felt like he was in the trenches again. They were in this fight together. More than in the past, he was careful to show his strength even though some days he'd rather just lie down on the floor and sleep away the nausea. He smiled where before he might've avoided someone's gaze.

There was something to it, something Franks had mentioned: "Life is a whole lot fuller when you stop thinking about yourself and start serving others."

And he was right.

There was the day the woman next to Elmore almost fell to the floor. She'd fallen asleep, and her frail body slipped before anyone else noticed. Thankfully he did. He pulled out his IV and hopped up from his chair.

When the woman woke up in his arms, they both laughed, even though blood squirted in tiny spews from where the IV had been – a gruesome scene with dark humor and strange camaraderie.

From that day on, she called him her hero. Funny. There it was again. Four letters of little consequence smashed together to make a word that felt earth shattering: hero.

He was no hero. He knew that. Sgt. Franks had known that. They were just ordinary people doing the occasional extraordinary thing because they had no choice but to do it. But that made Elmore think. An "extraordinary thing" was nothing more than something just outside the norm – something that made people feel needed and cared for.

So he focused more now. He learned the names of his ill comrades, talked to them and their families. They suffered together, but they took solace in the fact they weren't alone. They might one day be covered by a linen sheet, but this day, this twenty-four hours, they were part of something, no matter how small.

"They like you," Sam said one day.

He'd just said goodbye to another new friend, a young man in his twenties who'd come in looking like the Grinch but who now had the air of a man set on the right path.

"Who?" Elmore said, picking up a golf magazine lying on the table next to him.

"All of them."

"Oh? You took a survey?"

"No, dummy. Haven't you noticed?"

He had but he didn't want to let on. Better to let Sam think that she'd seen it first. She was observant, almost as much as Elmore, but she still had that dusting of youth that colored her observations.

"Have you thought about Sunday dinner?" he asked.

They'd talked about having Sgt. Franks and some of the other Marines over for a meal. Sort of a thank you. Sam said it could be a family dinner to start the week off right. Elmore had to admit to her that he'd liked the sound of that.

But why her face now? Had she changed her mind?

"What is it, Sam?"

"I... well, I don't want you to be mad."

Mad? How could he be mad at this lovely thing? More and more he was thinking of her as family. He'd even looked into formalizing the arrangement. Better to take those steps before social services stepped in. They'd granted him temporary custody, considering his military status and the recommendation of some highly placed friends, but that wouldn't last forever. Eventually the system would catch up with them.

"I won't be mad, Sam. Tell me."

Sam fiddled with her hands, wriggled and squeezing. "I sort of made a call."

"And?"

The words came out in a gush, and it took him a few seconds to unscramble what she'd said.

"I told your son that you were dying. He'll be at the house on Sunday."

CHAPTER SEVENTY-THREE

Despite Sam's surprise announcement three days before, Elmore felt a deep calm that took him through the hours of each twenty-four. He did feel like a kid ticking down the minutes for his birthday, but he tamped down his eagerness as Sam helped plan their Sunday meal.

The first order of business had been to ask their previous guests for a rain check. They'd start family night the following weekend. It was an unspoken truth that this confrontation was between a father and his son.

Sunday came, gloomy and overcast as clouds threatened to dump on their gathering. Elmore busied himself in the kitchen. They were having one of Eve's recipes: fried chicken and mashed potatoes. It had been Oliver's favorite.

The time came late and yet too soon. Five o'clock on the dot. No car in the drive.

Another ten minutes went by and still nothing.

"Maybe he got stuck in traffic," Sam said hopefully.

"Maybe."

But Elmore was starting to have that sinking feeling. His son wasn't coming. How could he blame the boy? He hadn't been a father. Not a real one. He'd played one until times got tough.

Had they really gotten tough? What was the one-sided argument about? Elmore didn't care. He was getting better. His spirits were in reverse proportion to his spiraling health. He and the porcelain king in the bathroom had become fast friends, but he didn't let that get him down. There was so much to do. So many people to touch. He'd started making at least one phone call each day. He chose an old friend from random and just called them. It was so out of character that the first couple of contacts had felt like an out-of-body experience.

But every call had turned out right. Not just right. Perfect. It was as simple as asking, "How have you been?"

Usually there was some hesitation. They knew him as Silent Nix, a man of few words.

What did make him smile, hell, it made him do flips inside, was when they actually started talking. And what fantastic conversations they had. They talked about their shared past. Sometimes they talked of loved ones now gone. Many talked of Eve, and what a treasure she was in their lives. Elmore felt like he was getting to know her all over again.

Now, here he was, waiting for his son. He was so full of hope, the thought that things might not go his way hadn't even entered the realm of possibility.

And yet, here it was. Reality slapping him in the face again.

"I should call him," Sam said.

Elmore didn't stop her. Luckily, Sam went to another room. He heard the mumbles through the walls and then the elevated voice from the far side of the house.

Sam came back in the room, face painted in red. "Men," she huffed.

"What happened?"

She didn't answer, but stomped around the living room, lost in thought.

Then she stopped in mid stride. "Get your keys."

Elmore had that sinking feeling again. Sam was already making her way to the garage like a running back taking on the opposing defensive line.

"Where are we going?"

"Elmore Thaddeus Nix, it's time for me to make something happen."

And the die was cast ‐ a wonderful, bold, caring die thrown in the center of life's ring.

Even though the fear had returned, Elmore found himself smiling, and then following Sam out to the car.

CHAPTER SEVENTY-FOUR

Lefts and rights they took, Sam guiding them via the GPS on her new phone. They'd gone maybe twenty miles. Elmore couldn't tell. He never went to this side of town. There were larger homes here, yards tended to perfection. Kids played, fathers threw balls while mothers and daughters chatted on porches. It was like driving into a Norman Rockwell painting.

"That's it," Sam said, pointing to the rambling one-story up ahead. The place was glorious in understated simplicity. Not a blade of grass out of place.

Elmore pulled into the drive. Two cars, both high-end sedans, had recently been washed. The red wash bucket still sat on the side of the drive. The poof sponges perched on the bucket's ledge, drying in the sun. Just like Elmore had taught his son. Always the same. Two sponges. One for each of them.

"Attack it from opposite ends before the water dries," Elmore remembered saying. In the early days, Oliver couldn't reach the top of the car so they had done sort of a revolving job of washing the family car.

"Are you gonna put the car in park?"

Elmore looked over at Sam. She was serious. Dead determined.

"Right."

He put the car in park just as the same little boy from the café ran out the front door, chased by the girl. Both froze stock-still when they noticed the car in the drive.

"Dad! Visitors!" the little boy called over his shoulder, and then ran for the opposite side of the house, squealing, with his older sister in pursuit.

"I guess that's our cue," Elmore said.

"Come on."

"Yes, General," he said, easing out of the seat.

By the time they'd made it to the door, Oliver was standing there, perturbed to be sure.

"What are you..." was all he managed to get out before Sam played into him.

"Look, sweetheart, I don't care what you two have against each other, but when you promise to come over for dinner, you do it. Understand? That's the right way to treat a person." She stood with one hand on her hip, the textbook definition of sass. Elmore couldn't help but smile.

"I..." Oliver once again started to say. Cut off again by Sam.

"Uh uh. My dad took off when I was ten and my mom is dead. I would do anything to have dinner with either one of them." That seemed to deflate any coming retorts from Oliver, his body deflating an inch and a half.

"I'm sorry," he said.

"That's a start. Now, why don't you two go inside? I'll keep an eye on the kids."

"They're fine. Eve's old enough to..."

Sam's raised hand did the job this time. "I said go inside."

Not much to do now except take the order and go inside. So they did, Oliver holding the door for his father, though Elmore was sure he didn't want to.

"Let's go in the kitchen," his son suggested without making eye contact with Elmore.

The outside was glamorous in that old Hollywood way, when starlets frolicked with macho leading men. The inside was beautiful with a tad uptick. There were touches of New York, "gold-rimmed bric-a-brac", as Eve would've put it. Little knick-knacks adorning shelves and low-lying tables.

"Beautiful house," Elmore said, almost without realizing it.

"Jacob's an interior designer."

"He's very good."

Elmore wasn't lying. This Jacob knew his stuff.

They made it to the kitchen without any more chatter. There was the sound of giggling children from outside.

"Have a seat," Oliver said, taking a chair on the opposite end of the table, a long slab of wood that looked like it'd been reclaimed from a strapping redwood.

Elmore sat down, not sure what he might say. Sorry? I love you?

He needn't have worried. Oliver barreled in.

"What are you doing here?"

"To tell you the truth, I don't know."

"You don't know?"

Elmore pointed to the window, toward the shrieks of laughter.

"She made me come." He immediately regretted his choice of words.

Oliver didn't seem to notice, instead glancing toward the backyard, where the sound of playing had drifted.

"Please tell me she's not your girlfriend."

"Oh, no, it's nothing like that."

"How do you know her?"

"Met her at the grocery store."

That made Oliver laugh. Some of the tension left him. How Elmore loved that sound. It was his son, at least for a fleeting moment.

"At the grocery store?"

"Cross my heart," Elmore said, tracing an X over his chest.

They sat there for a while, just listening to the little boy laughing out loud, occasionally interrupted by a giddy yell from Sam.

"Did you say your daughter's name...?"

"It's Eve," Oliver said, without looking at his father.

"Did your mother know?"

"No."

"I love you, son."

Oliver froze. Then, as if he was shaking off an anaconda around his neck, he said, "You can't just come in here and say that."

"But I said it. And I don't want to go to my grave knowing that I didn't."

"It's just words, Dad. Love is a verb; didn't you ever hear that one?"

"I'm sorry."

Oliver turned away with a huff. "Stop that."

Elmore didn't have to search for the words now. They just came. They'd always been there, like a dusty forgotten potion to be drunk at just the right moment.

"It's never too late, son. I'm sorry. For everything. You have every right to hate me, and I understand if you don't want to forgive me. But I've... well, I've changed. I have cancer and I was shot. Let's just say I've had my wakeup call."

"You got shot?" Oliver asked, a hint of that old curiosity there, or was it concern? Elmore couldn't tell.

"I did."

"How'd it happen?"

Elmore told him everything. About how Sam disappeared, how he'd tracked her down. About the mother and her boyfriend. Oliver just sat there, like a movie producer listening to a screenplay being read aloud, ready to pass judgement, mulling over a thumb up or down.

"I'm making quite a name for myself at the hospital."

"I wondered why, you know, why you don't look so hot."

Elmore laughed. "That's an understatement. I really do look like death on a Triscuit."

Oliver let out a little laugh. "Mom used to say that."

"I can't seem to let go of those."

Go on, son, laugh some more, Elmore thought. He realized in those last couple years, before he'd left, Oliver hadn't done much laughing. He'd passed it off as a young man finding his way. But Elmore knew now, somehow, instinctively maybe, that there'd been more too it. There'd been an inner struggle. And then that day when he'd tried to tell them.

"I'm sorry, son."

"You said that already."

"I know. But I'll say that until the day I die if I have to. The day you left, it was my fault. Don't blame your mother. And don't blame yourself."

"I blamed you both."

"I know, but it was my fault."

And then, like someone, God maybe, reached down and sprinkled them with truth serum, Oliver said, "I was frustrated. I'd planned it all out, you know. I knew how I was going to tell you. In my head you were going to run around the table and give me a big hug. We'd go out to dinner or mom would make fried chicken and mashed potatoes." Oliver shook his head, the sadness rising to the surface. "It was stupid. I was stupid." His eyes snapped up. "I was just a kid. But I just thought..."

"Just thought what?"

"I just thought a father's love transcended any ideas of what a man is supposed to be, when that man is his son."

Elmore felt his old self threatening to cave in on itself. The old him. The coward. The quiet one.

No, he said to himself.

"I was not a real man myself. A real man loves his son no matter what." Elmore shook his head trying to find the right words. What would Eve say? Something perfect. Something so delicate that had the force of a titan's fist. "I messed up, son. It was all me. Yell at me if you want to. Say whatever you want. But I'm not letting you go again. I made that mistake once. I'm not doing it."

Oliver was breathing in heavy sucks of air now. Elmore couldn't tell if his son was going to leave the room or not. He didn't blame him. He'd never blamed him for a damned thing. He'd come into their lives like a streak from heaven. Wonderful. Beautiful. All theirs, and Elmore had thrown it away.

"You don't know what it was like."

"Then tell me, son."

Oliver looked up, tears in his eyes now. "I... I never hated you. That's what hurt the most. If I hated you, it would have been easy."

"I understand."

Oliver shook his head, hard, emphatically.

"No. That girl..."

"Sam."

"She lost her mother. If she can forgive, start over..."

Elmore's heart thudded with hope, so much that it felt

like his chest might explode. "Take all the time you need, son. I won't press you, I promise. And if it happens after I die, so be—"

The boy threw himself into his father's arms.

So many words he should've said over the years. *I'm sorry. I love you. That's wonderful.* Whether it was his generation, his upbringing, or just his innate stubbornness, he'd missed his chances.

No more, he told himself. No more.

Live.

"I love you, son." He couldn't stop saying 'son', not now. Not ever.

When the hug subsided, Oliver pulled himself away, avoiding his gaze, a touch of the old Nix stubbornness there – don't let them see you like that.

"You have my number," said Elmore.

Then he left, leaving Oliver to his thoughts. He didn't have the perfect parting words, and that didn't matter. He'd played it wide open, left it all out on the field. What more could he do? It was out of his hands.

There was a time when you worried about your choices, and another when you just had faith that things would take care of themselves. This was the latter.

Elmore looked up as the sun peeked out from behind the lazy clouds. It really was a glorious day, now. The rain was gone like a dazzling burst of life streaking through the heavens through every color in the world. He felt alive. He felt whole.

Sam ran up then, the boy and girl close on her heels. Elmore knelt down to introduce himself.

"Hi," he said.

"Hi," said the boy. "What's your name?"

"I'm Elmore. What's yours?"

"Elmo? Like the red monster?"

Elmore laughed. "Close. It's Elmore." He was careful to pronounce the R.

The boy's eyes lit up. "Oh. Okay."

"You didn't tell me your name."

The boy looked to his sister and then to the front door. Oliver was there looking on. He nodded to the boy.

"I'm Thaddeus, but everyone calls me Thad. You don't say the H."

The boy stuck out his hand, as confident as a Wall Street broker.

"It's a pleasure to meet you, Thad." Elmore somehow held it together. Somehow. "Now, I hope I see you again soon."

"Can you bring the big girl with you?" Thad was pointing at Sam.

Sam scooped him up in her arms, a ball of giggling arms and legs.

"Of course, I'll come back," then she glanced at the front door. "If it's okay with your dad."

Everyone looked at Oliver.

"Sure. How about next weekend, after we get back from seeing Uncle Pete?"

Thad put his arms in the air, the boxer who'd just taken down Mohammed Ali. "Yes!"

Sam put him down and Thad ran to the back of the house again.

"Oliver, honey," said Sam, "you maybe wanna cut down on their sugar intake?"

Oliver rolled his eyes with a light smile.

Finally, Elmore had his chance with the girl, Eve.

"Hi, Eve, I'm Elmore." He offered his hand.

"Hi," she said shyly. Her hand was soft, delicate.

"I sure am glad I got to meet you."

She offered a small smile, one of those where you could tell they weren't sure whether to agree or not. He didn't care.

"Eve. That's a beautiful name."

Then, to her surprise as much as Elmore's, she blurted, "It was your wife's name."

Elmore just smiled. "That's right. She would've loved to meet you too."

That's my granddaughter, Elmore thought, marveling at the fact that his family might just survive. *I have two granddaughters now.*

"Are you coming back next weekend?" Eve asked. There was something in her question. More than what she'd actually asked.

"As long as I'm welcome, I wouldn't miss it."

Eve looked back at her father, like she didn't want to ask a question she wasn't allowed to ask.

"Can we visit you some time, you know, to see where my grandma lived?"

Elmore caught his breath. "If it's okay with your dad, it's just fine with me."

Eve retreated to the backyard after giving Elmore one last smile, one last treat for his swelling heart.

"Thank you," Elmore said to his son.

A nod from Oliver, and warmth on his son's face.

Hope blossomed bigger now. And in that moment, more than before, Elmore knew he'd beaten cancer. Crushed it into nonexistence.

CHAPTER SEVENTY-FIVE

"You look like a kid running to Chuck E. Cheese," Sam noted the next morning as Elmore rushed to scoop up his car keys and get to the garage.

"I'm on a mission, Sam. We gotta kick cancer in the teeth."

And that's the attitude they both took. Through aches. Through the visits to the porcelain king. They did it together.

When Elmore went in for a routine check up on Friday, a day before their next visit with Oliver and clan, the nurse, who was usually gruff and all business, noted, "Mr. Nix, you sure look better today."

Elmore had looked in the mirror a half dozen times that morning. He knew there was nothing physically different. He was even down a couple more pounds. The muscles on his arms sagged like they'd popped and deflated. But he knew what she meant. He felt the fire again. Hot and growing.

"Thank you," he said simply. "And may I say that you look lovely today." The veteran nurse actually blushed. Ah, the power of words.

That day dragged by. Sam had done all she could to prepare. Not that there was much. The plan was to have a good old-fashioned cook out at Oliver's. His husband would be there, along with the kids, of course. Casual. Fun. Together at last.

But fate was a cruel mistress.

The call came at 3:28pm. Elmore remembered and always would.

"Hello?"

"Is this Elmore Nix?"

"Yes."

"Mr. Nix, this is Gloria Riddle. I'm a nurse at University Hospital."

Elmore's first thought was Oliver. Oh God, please not that.

He gulped down the fear as best he could.

"Yes?"

"Mr. Nix, you're listed as next of kin for a Mr. George Franks."

"Okay," was all he could get out.

"Mr. Nix, I think it's best if you visit your friend now."

"What happened?"

"Mr. Nix, he doesn't have much time."

That was all Elmore needed to hear. He thanked the nurse and ended the call.

Sam was with him then, her eyes searching his. How she'd grown. She had the look of a vet, someone who'd seen the worst that the enemy could give. Too young for that.

"It's Franks."

"Let's go," Sam said, grabbing his hand and leading him where he could go himself.

THEY SPOKE with the same nurse who'd called. Gloria was all spit and polish with a healthy sprinkle of compassion. Perfect for her unfortunate position delivering the news no one wanted to deliver.

They said their thanks and rushed to room 309.

"Maybe you should go in without me," Sam suggested as they approached the room of the dying. Elmore could smell it. It was all around them. The ICU, the place where so many come to die. Somehow, he'd pushed through the feeling, through the mist of death, as familiar as rain, as mud, as burning mortar.

"Are you okay?" Elmore asked Sam. Maybe she was scared after all.

"I'm fine, it's just that he might want to see you alone."

"Nonsense. Come on." This time he grabbed her hand and in they went.

The room was bare and sterile. Machines bleeped and blooped. The place seemed almost hallowed, where a breath out of place would be sacrilege.

Sgt. Franks' chest rose and fell in a steady rhythm. There was a line running into his arm, and that IV line was hooked to at least three bags that Elmore could see. No mask. That was a good sign, or was it? He couldn't remember. No, that wasn't right; it was the tube down the throat that was bad. No tube down the throat but one disappearing into the old Marine's left nostril.

"Should we sit?" Sam asked.

"Go ahead," Elmore said, making his way to the edge of the bed.

He was looking for some sign of life, something that his friend was still there, mentally at least. The nurse said the doctor and his staff would give them the full run down. No doctor. So no answer.

"Franks," Elmore said, placed his hand on his friend's shoulder.

Sgt. Franks let out a little cough that turned into a full-blown heave. Elmore listened for the rattle, the 'death rattle' they called it.

It took a few coughs to clear and then the eyes came open, bloodshot but all Franks.

"You made it," he said.

"They called."

"Good. At least someone can do their job around here."

"So..."

"You're wondering why I'm here?"

"You were fine. I mean, we just saw you."

Franks nodded, glanced over at Sam. "How are you, young lady?"

"Fine."

"Did I mess up dinner?" There was the famous Franks grin.

"Big time," Sam said with a soft smile.

"We'll have to reschedule," said the old man.

He wasn't gonna get to it but Elmore was. "Franks, what the hell happened?"

Franks shrugged, which set off a fresh set of coughs. When he caught his breath again he said, "Liver's done."

"Why can't you get a new one?"

Franks leveled him with a glare that basically said Elmore was behind on the story.

"You don't think I already tried that?"

Now Elmore's 'seldom-seen' temper spiked. "Why the hell didn't you tell me? We could've tried something. Made calls. Jesus, Franks, you've been like a fath—"

Franks' tight grin cut through Elmore's anger. "There's the

Marine. Hold onto that, Nix. Never lose the fire. The ones that lose the fire are the first to die. You know that."

Elmore steadied his breath. "Yes."

"Gee," said Franks, with barely a breath of his own, "I wonder who taught you that."

"You did, you salty old bastard."

"That's right. And I didn't say it just to hear myself squawk. So yeah, my liver's shot. Too much boozing. Funny isn't it. I kicked the habit and then the habit kicked me."

"There's gotta be something."

"Full body shut down. They've got a phrase for it, but I like 'shut down' better. Sounds like my battery's finally running out. Now that I think about it, maybe they should call it decommissioning. I kinda like that, like the old battle-ships dragged into mothballs."

"Tell me what I can do," Elmore said.

This man, this monolith who'd been the pillar of strength and courage, this Marine's Marine, how could he be dying?

"You're here, aren't you?"

"I am."

"Then that's it."

"What about the others? Should I call—?

Franks' response was curt, almost a rebuke.

"No. Just you. And Sam of course." He smiled at Sam.

"But when I was in the hospital, you called up the reserves. You very well almost got us kicked out of the hospital."

"Sure. But that was for you. Me, I'm a different bird, Nix. And besides, I don't want them to see me this way."

"Come on. Let me make a couple calls. You can't—"

"This is my death, not yours. You want me to issue a direct order?"

Elmore wanted to shake the man. Before he could say another word, Franks winced in pain, his face going a ghastly shade of gray.

"I don't have much time." As if to accentuate that point, one of the machines made a whooping sound, like the most dangerous of alarms. It quieted after a moment, but not before a nurse poked her head in to make sure everything was A-OK.

When it was just the three of them again, Franks went on. "Remember your last day in Vietnam?"

Elmore didn't want to think about that but nodded anyway.

"It's still the same. You remember that."

And just like that, Elmore's mind cascaded back through the years, through the jungle and past the pain. Back to a time that life forgot.

THEY SAT on the edge of a cliff, a click and half outside of the wire. They shouldn't have been there, but who was going to tell Sgt. Franks and Cpl. Nix they couldn't do something? All the guards had done was hand them an extra magazine apiece and tell them to watch out for VC.

But Franks had a feel for the land now. Nix knew he'd never had that. He understood war, its savagery, the lay of the battlefield. But like a Sioux warrior on the plains, Franks seemed to know every blade of grass, every oversized leaf on the rain-soaked trees.

So here they were, sitting in the most beautiful place Elmore Nix had ever seen. The cliff they sat on was part of a three-quarter circle high above the ground. Across the way, waterfalls overflowed with the beginnings of the monsoon season. Birds chirped from unseen perches and the world settled into a peace untouched by war just outside the boundaries of this strange oasis.

"What is this place?"

Franks took a long drag from his cigarette and then passed it to Nix. Blue smoke streamed out as he answered. "Found it on one of my first patrols. Locals say it's some kind of holy place. We probably shouldn't even be smoking here. Nobody at headquarters knows what it is. Even asked the colonel once and he said it was off limits. Guess both sides just agreed to let it lie."

"Amazing," Elmore said, soaking it all in. This place, this paradise, how had it stood through the pounding of artillery and the scorching of napalm?

He had one day left until they shipped him back to the States. He'd thought about just making a run for it, hiding in the bush. But what would that accomplish? He could live off the land, some mysterious figure saving American units until the war was over. Just a pipe dream. Stupid kid stuff.

Besides, he had a feeling that Franks had sensed his moves. Since the brass had told him he was going home, Franks had been on him like a suicide watch. He would never do that, but his insides wanted to do something. Like an athlete retired before his time, the warrior spirit in Nix burned, daring the world to put it out.

"So, you're going home tomorrow," Franks said, snapping him out of his reverie.

"Yeah."

"Wish I was going with you."

"Bullshit."

Franks took the cigarette and inhaled deeply, burning the end red. "I'd leave right now if they let me."

"Bullshit," Nix repeated.

"You already said that. And yeah, I'd go in a heartbeat."

"But our Marines..."

Franks sat up, leveled Nix with the cool stare of every salty veteran who'd stared down the mortar tube of eternity.

"You think you're special."

The simple words stung like a harpoon tearing through Nix's chest.

"No, I..."

Franks laughed, breaking his serious facade.

"You're not alone, Nix. I thought I was special too. It took a gunny bleeding out in my arms to tell me different. Old bastard gave me shit every day for two months. Mother-fucker looked sixty years old. You know how old he was when he died? Barely thirty." Franks shook his head in wonder. "War does crazy shit to us, Nix. Remember that. Anyway, back to you being special. I'll tell you what that gunny with no legs told me. He said, 'The Corps will replace you in a New York minute.' That's what he said, honest to Skippy. There are hundreds, maybe thousands of kids who don't know they're the next Cpl. Nix. How's that make you feel?"

"You're wrong."

Nix could hold the old salt's gaze now.

"You really think so? I was a DI at PI before this shitshow of a war. You know how many boots I tore down and built up again? The big green machine's been doing it for hundreds of years and they'll keep doing it hundreds of years after we're gone. We're not special." Another long drag, then the words came out more pronounced, and even in the moment, even with all the anger swirling in Nix's head, he still recognized the sanctity of the coming words.

"We're not special, but we were given a gift. We made it, or at least we made it so far. We've seen the worst of what life has to offer. And now you, lowly Corporal Nix, you get the golden ticket home and you don't want to go." Franks snorted, stubbed out the cig on his boot, and stuffed the butt into his breast pocket. "This..." he spread his arms, motioning to the glory that was the world all around them. "This is our gift." Then he poked his index finger into Nix's chest, and then into his own. "And this, this they can never take away from us. You think we ever would've met in the real world? No god dammed way. I was halfway to jail before the Corps caught up with me. Mama's green machine gave me a second chance, even though I fought it every step of the way. So here it is, Nix. The Corps, the world, hell, call it God if you want, they're all giving you a second chance. Vietnam chewed you up and now it's spitting you back out. Are you gonna take that chance?"

Nix didn't have an answer. He obviously never thought of his situation that way. He'd been so tied up in the unfairness of it all. He was being torn from his unit, from the only friends he had left, his only family.

That's when the question slipped out, so simple, so innocent. "How do I do it?"

Because, he really didn't know. How did he leave the only thing he thought he knew and go back to a world that probably would never understand him? He'd heard the rumors, the letters from back home. They were protesting more now. Returning veterans were no better than war criminals. What was he supposed to do, just take it? No, he couldn't. He'd been trained to fight, trained to strike back.

But Franks' words stretched between them, enveloped Nix's heart and let him take the next step.

"How do you do it? You *live*, Nix. You just live. That's how you give it back and give the world the finger at the same time. *You just fucking live.*"

ELMORE THADDEUS NIX, once Marine Corporal, stared down at his dying friend who was smiling now.

"Eve told me the same thing."

Franks flashed that Cheshire smile. "Of course, she did. She was smarter than you."

Elmore smiled at this, and then looked at his friend with puzzlement. "But you—"

Franks' smile was wider now. "Never met her? Of course, I did. Who do you think told her you were in New York? I told her to take care of you. And she did."

There were tears in both Marines' eyes now.

"She never told me."

"Why should she? Anyway, I told her not to. Besides, I knew I'd come home and have no one. I couldn't bear the thought of that happening to you. And look at me. I drank myself into the grave." He looked down at the tubes attached to his arm. "Took a little longer than I thought, but I did it."

How could it be? Elmore knew every detail of the day he'd met Eve. It was a chance encounter. That's even what Eve had said.

"Why hadn't you reached out sooner? Dammit, the times we could've had."

"C'mon, Nix, are you that thick? I had to let you live it out yourself. At least until it was time to swoop in and save you. Can't you see that, Nix? You'll always be my brother. I'd give you my liver if it was any good."

They both laughed at that then Franks foundered into a coughing fit. He looked worse now. Elmore saw it coming. Too close, that hand of death.

"So you take life by the balls and you run with it, Nix. Don't let me down, you hear?"

Elmore nodded. Words would've let the cascade of tears flow. So he just nodded over and over again. Until his friend faded.

So long, brother. I'll keep my promise.

CHAPTER SEVENTY-SIX

The funeral was a simple affair made grand by the sheer size of the entourage streaming in behind Elmore Nix. They filed in like they first filed off the bus at Parris Island and MCRD San Diego. Some had beer bellies of age. Others were pushed along in wheelchairs they'd be strapped to until the end. But they were Marines, all. Brothers. Once young. Once untouchable. Once blazed and tested in war. The world had tried to break them. Some had been broken and then been mended back together, by friends, by family, by God.

Now here they were, cherishing the memory of another comrade gone, but not forgotten.

Elmore still held the tiny sheet of paper they'd found on the table next to the hospital bed. Written in scratchy ink it read:

Nix, I don't want a fancy funeral. All I want is for you boys to tell some funny stories and remember when we were all together. Then I want you to go out and make this world better. God bless you all. I'll miss you. I'll see you on the other side.

Franks, Sgt. USMC

Elmore couldn't help but smile at the thought of his friend guarding the gates of heaven, patrolling the hallowed kingdom's streets just like they'd sung in the Marine's Hymn.

"It's a beautiful day," Sam said, now beside him as they took their spots around the grave site. A pile of dirt lay ready; the casket soon to be lowered.

"It is," Elmore said, unable to keep the emotion from his voice. This wasn't his friend's soul getting ready to be shut for all eternity. It was merely another hollow vessel left for mortal memory. But he found it hard to think of tomorrow. He was scared. Franks had been one of the rocks in his life. As long as the stalwart Marine was alive, things were right with the world.

It's your time now, he told himself. Eve had told him that and then Franks. They knew. They'd always seen it in him. Even Sam, in her youth, saw something in Elmore Thaddeus Nix that the aging man never saw in himself. He'd assumed the mantle of a humble worker, plodding through life trying to do the right thing, keeping his head bent to the Earth.

That was over now. He was here, staring into the eyes of his comrades, brothers in arms, friends. There were smiles, some grim, others cheery – like they'd arrived for a reunion. Or a birthday. Maybe that's exactly what this was. Their birthday, Elmore's birthday. A new day.

They listened as the pastor said his words, adding in a quip here and there like Franks had demanded in his will. Just like him to run his own funeral. There were laughs, of course, and the requisite tears. But for the most part, the entire affair was uplifting, a fitting tribute to a man they'd admired in their youth and kept as a symbol of strength and determination throughout their lives. Yes, that was Sgt. Franks. Marine. Their Marine.

There were stories. Some were risqué. Some were hilarious. They erupted in spurts from the crowd surrounding the grave. Laughter, God-gifted, sweet and fitting.

And then it was over. No more goodbyes. On to live, together, apart, on to the horizon.

Elmore was the last to leave, watching as the cemetery workers began the task of final burial.

Sam was waiting by the car when he was ready. "Thanks for letting me come."

"What do you mean 'letting' you come?" Elmore said, wrapping her in a hug. "He wanted you here. *I* wanted you here. Come on. Let me tell you about the time Franks showed me how to drink a whole beer through a straw."

CHAPTER SEVENTY-SEVEN

Their lives settled into a sort of rhythm. Treatment. Recovery. Rinse. Repeat.

Oliver had, of course, understood about his father's inability to join them for their scheduled dinner. They'd postponed the gathering until after Franks' burial. And then there was a family vacation to plan around.

Now the day was upon them again. Elmore didn't know for sure, couldn't until the doctor told him, but he felt stronger. Not physically. Damn that treatment. It took more out of him than a bout of malaria. But mentally, by measuring his soul, he felt more alive than he had in years. There was so much to do. His Marine buddies needed help in every conceivable way. Some afternoons he spent hours on the phone, just talking with retirees who had no one else to talk to. There were the visits to friends nearby, and ones within easy driving distance. His schedule was fuller now than it ever had been in his working days. And he loved it. Serving others kept him from thinking about his own predicament. Take that, CANCER!

That's the attitude he took with him on that late Saturday

afternoon as he and Sam drove to Oliver's. When they arrived, young Thad ran to the car and wasted no time pulling Sam out.

"I built a fort in the backyard. You have to come see!" he said to her.

"Aw jeez, here we go on the Pop Tart train to hell," she whispered as the kid dragged her off.

Elmore carried the pie they'd bought at the grocery store. Neither he nor Sam knew how to bake. It was something they'd learn together someday. For now, they'd rely on the experts.

Oliver met him at the door. No hugs were offered. Too soon for that. At least this time he looked relaxed, or at least at ease.

"Welcome back," Oliver said.

What I wouldn't give to have him call me dad again, Elmore thought.

"We brought a pie, store bought."

"Thanks." Oliver took the pie and ushered his father in the door.

Elmore smelled the smoke from the grill when he stepped inside, along with whatever side dishes were cooking in the kitchen.

"Looks like Thad found a friend," Oliver said, making his way to the kitchen. "He couldn't stop asking for Sam."

"She complains but she really loves it."

"Are you going to adopt her?" Oliver asked without turning. The question floored Elmore.

"I hadn't really thought about it."

"You should. Who knows what would happen to her if she goes back in to the system. I could help, if you want."

There was compassion in his son's voice now, some innocence that Elmore remembered from Oliver's youth.

"Sure. I mean, I'd appreciate that. I don't have the faintest idea of what I'm doing."

That's when Oliver turned and faced him, pie still in hand.

"You're doing the right thing, Dad."

Elmore couldn't help the tears from coming.

Oliver noticed. Nothing else to be said. Wonderful silence.

"Come on," he said after a moment. "Eve's almost done with the salad."

The cookout was silently added to the growing list of the best days in Elmore's life. Oliver's husband, Jacob, kept the conversation going. He owned a boutique interior design firm in town, and the ease with which he talked made Elmore think that he was very good with his clientele.

The only one who didn't partake in the conversation was Eve. She ate quietly, occasionally sneaking glances at Elmore, who pretended not to notice. He didn't want to embarrass her. He knew Oliver noticed, because of the way he kept looking at his daughter like he was surprised by her quiet tongue.

"That was delicious," Elmore declared when the meal was over.

"Yeah, that was really great. Thanks for letting me come," Sam said, looking like she'd just hopped off a carnival ride.

"You're part of the family now, Sam. You better get used to it," Jacob said. The married couple shared a look, silent consent that this would indeed happen again.

"Dad, what about dessert?" Thad asked.

"I'll get it," Eve said, quick to be out of her chair.

"I'll help," Elmore said.

She nodded at him, one of those shy little things that only a girl can give.

Off they went, Elmore with an armful of plates.

The dessert was Elmore and Sam's pie added to a cornucopia of fruit piled high on a clear platter.

"Thad loves strawberries," Eve said. The only words she'd said without prompting during their visit.

"What about you?" For some reason, Elmore was having a hard time finding the words. He wanted to make a good impression, and it was more than just the fact that this precious child shared his wife's name.

"I don't know," Eve said, eyes glued to where she was replacing a blueberry that had tumbled off the mountain that had been so carefully crafted.

Say something, Elmore thought, when the silence felt like it might stretch to the moon.

"I'll bet you like pineapple," he said.

Her head whipped his way. "How did you know?"

Elmore tapped the side of his head.

"I've got special powers. Didn't your dad tell you?"

Her eyes scrunched together, unbelieving. "No, you don't."

He was about to go along with the charade, cross his heart and hope to die. All that kiddie nonsense. But he stopped. Something in the room had changed like a subtle shift in the temperature, only it was more than that. Like the pressure had let up, and that's when he knew his wife was there, urging him to say what he really wanted to say. So he did.

"You're right I don't. I'm just your ordinary, run-of-the-mill old person."

She let out the tiniest giggle at that. "Then how did you know about the pineapple?"

Keep the emotions in check, Corporal.

"My Eve, your grandmother, she loved pineapples. So I just guessed. Maybe it has to do with the name, Eve. I remember the time we spent a week in Hawaii, and all she ate for breakfast was pineapples. Seven straight days. Didn't think it was the least bit strange. I thought she was going to turn yellow!"

No giggle this time, just wide eyes.

"Is it okay, I mean, do you think you could tell me about her, when we have more time?"

That's when he knew it would be okay, that his life would go on. He'd fight tooth and nail for every last second with this child, with her brother and their parents. For the first time he felt whole, even if the doctors were telling him different. Damn them anyway and fuck the cancer. He'd beat it, odds be damned. What did they know?

His smile lit up the room now. It chased every ounce of shadow and ill will away in a ten-block radius. "Eve, it would be my pleasure. Now come on. I'm sure your brother would like his strawberries."

CHAPTER SEVENTY-EIGHT

"Well, I'm not sure what else to say..." the doctor's face was all but calm. Elmore had known him for years, had been through good times and bad, but had never seen him so flustered. "Your scans came back clean," the doctor said, pretty muted blurting out the words, confusion still there.

"You don't seem happy about that, Doc," Elmore deadpanned.

More fluster and bluster behind the vaunted desk.

"I'm sorry, Elmore, it's just that... well, how can I say this without sounding like a complete ass..."

"Just say it."

Years of confidence blew out of the man as he exhaled in a long drawn out breath. "Your last tests, I told you I was optimistic. Well, I was, but that was because you looked," searching for the words again, "well, you looked good."

"But my tests said otherwise."

The doctor looked up at his friend. "I'm sorry, Elmore. Sometimes a modicum of truth is better than a dagger to the chest."

"I understand."

"You do?"

"Sure."

The doctor was searching again, only this time it felt to Elmore that he was looking for hints of betrayal from his friend. A lie. It had to be there, the doctor must be thinking.

Finally, another huff and then, "You've got me then. I don't understand how you're taking this so calmly. I'd expect you to be kicking and screaming, maybe even driving to find the first malpractice lawyer between here and home. Hell, I could give you a list if you'd like."

Now that made Elmore smile. He'd been holding it in. No sense making it easy on the trusted physician. You're not great friends unless you give a little grief every once in a while. Keeps you on your toes. Keeps you humble.

"Now, Ted, you know me better than that."

"Well, sure, Elmore, but..."

"No buts about it. You said it yourself. I'm on the mend. I feel healthy. My appetite is back. Life couldn't be better."

"But...?"

Elmore stood, holding up a hand as he rose.

"Ted, you do good work. I trust you. But in this case, you didn't do it alone."

"I've seen a lot of things in my life, Elmore. A lot of good, but a lot of bad too. Had to tell people some awful truths."

"I wouldn't have your job for all the money in the world," Elmore said, and he meant it. A good doctor was worth more than his weight in gold. You find a doctor that's not only good at his craft, but takes the time to really care for a patient (despite what the insurance companies pay), now that was a doctor Elmore could stand behind. That was Ted. House calls without getting paid. Phone calls despite the inability to pay.

Elmore knew. The community knew. That's why they kept coming.

"Okay. Then tell me this, Mr. Elmore Nix. I'll shoot you straight because I know you can take it. You were on your way out. Your ticket was punched. Sure, treatment could've given you some time, but there's never a guarantee with these things. So, tell me, in your expert opinion – because I now believe you are an expert in such things – tell me how you got fixed? How are you walking out of my office with a clean bill of health?"

The man was truly flummoxed. Elmore almost felt bad for him. With a now-familiar twinkle in his eye, Elmore grinned at his friend. "I finally learned how to live, Ted. That's it. Plain and simple."

And with that, he left the doctor, and went to tell his family the good news. They were all outside on the playground: Sam, Oliver, Jacob, Eve, and little Thad.

He was pretty sure Sam had known all along. She was a spitfire, that one. She'd gone as far as to tell the social worker to her face that even if the state didn't see fit to let Elmore adopt her, she'd tattoo his name on her forehead, "Elmore Thaddeus Nix," she'd said, sounding out every syllable, if they denied the request. "Nobody else would want me after that." And Elmore was pretty sure the social worker had believed her.

But it was young Eve who'd really known. It had been the night before. They'd come over for movie night, Sam's idea. Now that Elmore had a monstrosity of a television (again, courtesy of Sam's not so subtle suggestion), they'd settled in to watch *Ben-Hur*, the original with Charlton Heston. It was Oliver's favorite and Elmore's too. Just as the beginning credits rolled, Eve had leaned over and whispered in her grandfather's ear, "You're gonna be okay, grandpa. Grandma told me in my dreams last night."

And it was all Elmore could do not to cry. Because she was there. They were all there. His family. Finally. They were whole. And he felt whole. For the first time, maybe ever.

No, that wasn't true. There'd been that day in Central Park, when the clouds parted and God gave him his Eve. She with all her spunk and charm and he with all his pent-up anger and hurt. They'd come together as if in a dream, a match for the ages. A miracle in plain sight. The mismatched pair stuck together in masterful perfection.

So, when Elmore Thaddeus Nix walked outside the next morning, the sun casting its magnificent rays upon him, like a kissed blessing, all he could think to say to the heavens was, "Thank you."

What a blessing it was to be able to say that.

I hope you enjoyed this story.
If you did, please take a moment to write a review ON AMAZON. Even the short ones help!

GET A FREE COPY OF THE CORPS JUSTICE PREQUEL SHORT STORY, *GOD-SPEED*, JUST FOR SUBSCRIBING AT CG-COOPER.COM

Follow me on Facebook HERE and join my private Facebook group HERE. It's a great place to have chats with Team Cooper.

Oh! And don't forget to keep turning for the links to the rest of my books.

ALSO BY C. G. COOPER

The Corps Justice Series In Order:

Back To War

Council Of Patriots

Prime Asset

Presidential Shift

National Burden

Lethal Misconduct

Moral Imperative

Disavowed

Chain Of Command

Papal Justice

The Zimmer Doctrine

Sabotage

Liberty Down

Sins Of The Father

A Darker Path

Corps Justice Short Stories:

Chosen

God-Speed

Running

The Daniel Briggs Novels:

Adrift

Fallen

Broken

Tested

The Tom Greer Novels

A Life Worth Taking

The Spy In Residence Novels

What Lies Hidden

The Alex Knight Novels:

Breakout

The Stars & Spies Series:

Backdrop

The Patriot Protocol Series:

The Patriot Protocol

The Chronicles of Benjamin Dragon:

Benjamin Dragon – Awakening

Benjamin Dragon – Legacy

Benjamin Dragon - Genesis

Stand Alone Novels

To Live

ABOUT THE AUTHOR

C. G. Cooper is the USA TODAY and AMAZON BESTSELLING author of the CORPS JUSTICE novels (including spinoffs), The Chronicles of Benjamin Dragon and the Patriot Protocol series.

Cooper grew up in a Navy family and traveled from one Naval base to another as he fed his love of books and a fledgling desire to write.

Upon graduating from the University of Virginia with a degree in Foreign Affairs, Cooper was commissioned in the

United States Marine Corps and went on to serve six years as an infantry officer. C. G. Cooper's final Marine duty station was in Nashville, Tennessee, where he fell in love with the laid-back lifestyle of Music City.

His first published novel, BACK TO WAR, came out of a need to link back to his time in the Marine Corps. That novel, written as a side project, spawned many follow-on novels, several exciting spinoffs, and catapulted Cooper's career.

Cooper lives just south of Nashville with his wife, three children, and their German shorthaired pointer, Liberty, who's become a popular character in the Corps Justice novels.

When he's not writing or hosting his podcast, Books In 30, Cooper spends time with his family, does his best to improve his golf handicap, and loves to shed light on the ongoing fight of everyday heroes.

Cooper loves hearing from readers and responds to every email personally.

To connect with C. G. Cooper visit
www.cg-cooper.com

52028695R00163

Made in the USA
Middletown, DE
06 July 2019